Ghost Doll and Jasper

Ghost Doll and Jasper

Fiona McDonald

SKY PONY PRESS
New York

Sky Pony Press books may be purchased in bulk at special discounts for sales promotion, corporate gifts, fund-raising, or educational purposes. Special editions can also be created to specifications. For details, contact the Special Sales Department, Sky Pony Press, 307 West 36th Street, 11th Floor, New York, NY 10018 or info@skyhorsepublishing.com.

Sky Pony® is a registered trademark of Skyhorse Publishing, Inc.®, a Delaware corporation.

Visit our website at www.skyponypress.com.

10 9 8 7 6 5 4 3 2 1

Library of Congress Cataloging-in-Publication Data

McDonald, Fiona.
Ghost Doll and Jasper / Fiona McDonald.
pages cm
Summary: In search of a loving home, a ghost doll, accompanied by her cat companion, tries to navigate the modern city and avoid capture by an evil scientist.
ISBN 978-1-62087-174-4 (hardcover : alk. paper) [1. Ghosts–Fiction. 2. Dolls--Fiction. 3. Cats–Fiction. 4. Friendship–Fiction. 5. Home–Fiction. 6. City and town life–Fiction.] I. Title.
PZ7.M47841774Gh 2012
[Fic]–dc23

2012027235

Printed in the United States of America

For my mother, Win McDonald

Chapter 1

In an old part of town,

on a long forgotten street,

in a house with no door,

full of dark and musty corners, lay a dirty, battered doll.

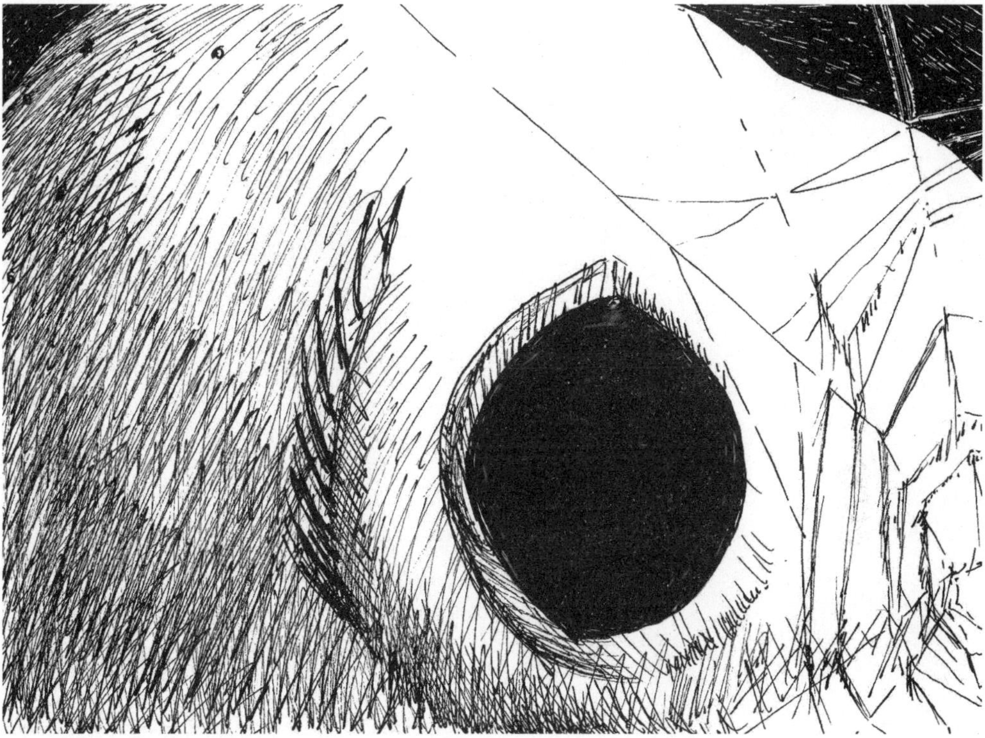

How many years she'd been there, no one could tell. Spiders had covered her with cobwebs and dust lay like a blanket over her, keeping her warm. Mice crept across the floor and sometimes scuttled over her body, plucking her hair for their nests. Beetles nibbled her fingers and toes while the winter wind blew dead leaves and empty food packets through the door. But the doll lay still and uncomplaining, oblivious to everything.

Until one night . . .

. . . when a star exploded and sent its powerful fragments showering through the atmosphere. One tiny spark fell through a hole in the roof and landed on the doll's forehead.

It sank through the fragile plastic—she had been one of the first to be made in that marvelous new material—and deep within the empty eye sockets, old memories flickered into life.

The doll awoke.

What a sleep! So many dreams; how refreshing. She jumped up and spun around, light as the stardust she now was.

The house was dark. Where was everybody? Where was her little girl? The doll wanted to share the dreams she'd had of flowers and picnics and tea parties with her.

The rooms smelled cold and damp and lonely. The furniture was gone. The wallpaper hung in strips off the walls. How long had she slept? The doll went upstairs. The bedrooms were empty. No beds, no curtains, no toys. What had happened? The doll flitted from room to room. In Lucy's room, there was still the old wardrobe with its heavy mirror. The doll approached slowly—a suspicion had been growing in her. The wardrobe was bare, and there was not a sign that a little girl had once used it. No party dresses, hats, shoes, or pink hair ribbons.

The long mirror was dark, reflecting back the cobwebs and the dim corners of the room. The doll stood before it and gasped. She was different. She was white and shining. Her legs had disappeared and her body was transparent. She'd become a ghost!

Crystal tears streamed down her pale cheeks, and she crumpled to the floor like an old tissue. How had this happened? Why had she been left behind? And why was she awake now?

Then she heard it. Ever so quietly, something was walking around downstairs. Ghost Doll sprang from the floor and dashed to the top of the steps. She was floating! Zooming! No feet, no legs, and she could go fast and as silent as the dead. She couldn't help giggling; it was quite fun.

Ghost Doll peered over the rickety banister. Perhaps her girl had come back for her after all. She'd come back to find her special doll and take her to a new house. But there was no little girl standing in the room below. At first, Ghost Doll couldn't see anyone there. Then she heard the faint noise again, a slight movement, a gentle breath. In the far corner where she herself had been lying for so long, now lay a mangy black cat.

Just a cat, thought Ghost Doll, disappointedly. Looking for shelter perhaps. It certainly hadn't belonged to the family. Mother had been allergic to animals, so there'd never been one in the house. "Nasty, dirty things," Father had said. Ghost Doll had been inclined to agree with him, but she remembered how her little Lucy had wanted a pet so much. With that thought in mind, Ghost Doll silently drifted down the stairs.

The cat was busy cleaning its leg. Drops of something dark fell to the floor: blood. Ghost Doll felt a pang of sympathy for the cat. It was hurt.

"Kitty, kitty," she called. The cat whirled around in a blur of black fur and sharp claws. Ghost Doll crept closer. "Kitty, kitty," she called again. "It's all right, I won't hurt you."

The cat backed further into the corner, its back arched and its tail swelled out like a toilet brush, hissing and spitting. Ghost Doll could see more blood oozing out of a long gash on its upper leg. The poor cat had been in a fight.

"Come on, kitty," she coaxed, floating closer. The cat lashed out, and its paw sank through the doll's body. The cat cowered in fear. What was this new threat? he wondered. Ghost Doll reached out and put one finger on the tip of the cat's nose. Perhaps a speck of stardust lingered on her finger, because suddenly the cat relaxed. The two stared at each other for a whole minute.

"What on earth are you?" asked the cat.

"What do you mean, 'what on earth are you?' I'm a doll," said Ghost Doll, annoyed.

"Uh, not meaning to be rude," said the cat, "but you are a bit see-through."

"Well, I'm rather old, I think," said the doll. "And what are you doing in my house?"

"Your house?" said the cat. "I didn't think anyone lived here anymore."

"Well, I do," replied the doll. "Let's see your wounds. You happen to be dripping blood all over my wooden floor, and it will stain."

The cat gave her an odd look, but let Ghost Doll gently prod and poke him. She used spiderwebs to clean the cuts and bites.

"Well, I'll be off now," said the cat, limping towards the door.

"You can't go out like that," said the doll. "Your wounds will get infected, and you could freeze to death. Stay here, just for the night." The cat was hesitant, as if he didn't trust her.

"Don't suppose you've got anything to eat?" he asked.

"Mice? You'd have to catch them yourself," Ghost Doll replied.

"I'll just go to sleep then, if you don't mind." The cat looked around suspiciously. He curled around a couple of times, then made himself into a tight ball.

"Thanks for letting me stay," he said, and went to sleep.

Ghost Doll sat and watched him. She was a bit disappointed that the cat hadn't wanted to talk. After all those years of silence she thought it would be nice to catch up on the happenings of the world. Perhaps in the morning the cat would feel better and be more talkative. Ghost Doll sat as still as if she had been made of stone. The mice came out as usual, but when they saw both the shimmering figure and the sleeping cat, they tiptoed away as quickly as possible.

Chapter 2

That same night, in another part of town . . .

"Blast it!" yelled a man. He was tall and thin with a head like a large, boiled egg. His glasses were so thick that they magnified his eyes out of proportion to his face.

"Bring me the spanners."

A large creature, part animal, part machine, whirred across the tiled floor, pushing a metal tray on wheels. On the top lay an array of tools.

"Not those!" the man yelled at the creature. "The others, those ones." He waved towards the other corner of the room. The animal, possibly a dog, rolled towards the second cart, which held an almost identical set of tools, and pushed it over to his master.

"We have to get this finished," said the man as he tinkered with the large mass of metal and glass, bright knobs and levers. It looked like a large fish tank, only taller than it was long, and a bit like a shower stall.

"Is the telescope set?" the man asked after a final twist of a bolt.

"Yes, master," replied the dog. Its metal tail moved squeakily from side to side in an attempt to wag.

"You need an oil. Bring me the can. I can't afford a distraction when I'm working." The dog brought an oil can over and stood patiently while his master put a couple of drops onto his tail.

"There we are, good boy." The man patted the top of the dog's large, metallic head, then stood, wiping his hands on an oily rag while his oversized eyes looked up at the clock on the wall.

"Nearly time," he said. "Come, let's see where it lands." The man moved across the tiled floor to a brass telescope that stood before a large window. The town lay spread before him, a black silhouette against a darkening sky. Lights began to sprinkle their way across the town as people got ready for nighttime.

All of a sudden, a great ball of fire came hurtling across the sky, trailing a long, blazing tail. The man stood in awe. The exploding star whizzed over the town, and as it did so, gold flakes broke away from it and floated down into a street some distance away.

"Got it!" he shouted triumphantly. He scribbled down the general location of the fallen fragments. "No rush, the streets over that way are all deserted. They will be demolished very soon. No one knows what to do with stardust except me, so there is no hurry. We'll pick it up in the morning." With that, he went back to working on his fish tank in the corner, a large smile spreading across his face.

Chapter 3

Ghost Doll was at the window, watching the sun rise over the tumbling roofs of the houses surrounding her. She had not seen dawn break for a very long time, and she admired the great burning ball as it steadily rose, making the dark of the night flee before it.

The cat woke and tentatively stretched out a paw. He flinched with the pain of the wound, then carefully sat up and began licking himself.

"Hello," said Ghost Doll, turning from the window. "How are you feeling this morning?"

The cat looked up from his cleaning. "Stiff and sore," he said, and went back to washing his hind legs.

"What happened to you?" Ghost Doll wandered over and sat down in front of him, not too close, though, as she felt he was still not sure about her.

"Got into a fight."

"With what? Another cat?"

"Of course it was another cat," he answered without looking at her. "A big orange tom by the name of Murdo Nally."

Ghost Doll sat and watched, fascinated by the way the cat could twist and turn himself into such contortions while bathing. However, her own new form was vastly more flexible than her old one, which had been limited, being made of rigid plastic and having no elbows or knees.

"And what is your name?" Ghost Doll asked. She didn't want to keep calling him "cat" or nothing at all.

"Jasper," the cat said. "What's yours?"

Ghost Doll tried to remember. It had been a long time since anyone had called her anything.

"Well, sometimes I was called Dolly," she said at last. "But then I was Sweetie a lot of the time, or Darling, or You-Naughty-Girl—it all depended what my little girl Lucy was playing."

"So, what do I call you?"

"Well, I'm not sure. I don't like any of those names really, so just call me Ghost Doll until we think of something else."

Jasper looked at his new friend with his yellow-green eyes and tried to think of a more suitable name. He couldn't.

"Okay, Ghost Doll," he said. "What about breakfast?"

"Same problem as last night, I'm afraid," said Ghost Doll. Of course, she didn't need to eat. She had never needed to. However, she did remember the tea parties she'd had with Lucy. There had been cakes with pink icing and little sandwiches cut into triangles. Lemonade had fizzed into the doll-sized teacups, and milk had frothed in the jug. Ghost Doll felt a pang of sadness and realized she could almost understand what "hunger" meant.

"There is no food in the house," she said. "I think my people left a long time ago. There are still lots of mice, though."

"Oh well, it can't be helped," said Jasper, getting to his feet. "We should be going anyway."

"What do you mean?" asked Ghost Doll. "Why should we be going, and where? I don't need to eat, and this is my home. You go get some breakfast and then come back here. I thought we could talk."

Jasper stared at the doll.

"You don't know?" he said. "You haven't heard?"

"What?"

"This house is going to be demolished. Today. In an hour or so. We move or get smashed along with the bricks and mortar. You can't stay here. It will be horrible."

"This house is getting knocked down? Why?" Ghost Doll hovered in the morning sun, and if it were possible for a ghost to go even paler, Jasper would have sworn she had turned pure white with fear.

"There is a new shopping center planned for this area. All the old houses are being torn down. Three streets have already gone. It's a wonder you haven't heard the noise."

"I only woke up yesterday evening," said Ghost Doll. "Jasper, what shall I do? I don't want to live in a pile of rubble. And my little girl has gone. What do I do now?"

"I guess you'll have to come with me," he said finally. "We'll find a home for you, I'm sure we will." He said it confidently, but he had great doubts as to how he could help her.

A rumbling shook the house, and bits of plaster fell from the ceiling. Ghost Doll and Jasper fled to the doorway.

"What's that?" called Ghost Doll.

"The crane with the demolition ball on it, I'd say," replied Jasper. "Look, we'll have to go now before all the dust and dirt starts flying."

He dashed out the door into the street, Ghost Doll close behind him. As they raced up the road Ghost Doll saw the monster machines come growling towards them. She had never seen anything so frightening before. They were trucks of some kind, but they were so big, and their huge tires crushed things as they rolled over them: old tins, a wooden box, a broken chair that lay on its side, and even a couple of bricks that had fallen from someone's garden wall. It seemed as if these mechanical giants would eat everything in their path. Jasper was several feet ahead of her already. Ghost Doll realized there was nothing for her here now.

"Hang on!" she called. "Wait, I'm coming!"

The two disappeared around the corner before the great ball made its first blow.

Chapter 4

"Come, Dog," said the tall, thin man. His bald head was covered by a black felt hat, and a long scarf was wound around his scrawny neck. "Let's go hunting for stardust." The metal dog followed behind his master on caterpillar tracks, crawled down the stairs, and zoomed out the front door. The man had a black box slung from one shoulder. He pulled the door shut behind them. A small brass plate had a name engraved on it: Dr. J. Borsch—scientist and inventor. As the man moved away from the house, followed closely by the dog, he took the box in both hands, pulled an antenna out from the top, and turned several knobs on the side. The box let out a series of squeaks and crackles. Dr. Borsch adjusted the settings until the box began to emit a low, steady hum.

"Okay, Dog, I've got the location. Let's go." Scientist and creature went straight down the street, passing closed doors and curtained windows. The sun had only just risen and most people were still snuggled under blankets and quilts, sleeping soundly.

"We need to get over to the East Side before the demolition starts," said Dr. Borsch.

They strode across the intersection, ignoring the "No Walk" sign. Once or twice the pair passed someone opening a store, sweeping away the trash on the sidewalk from the day before. Smells of baked goods wafted over them. Dog lifted his metal nose to inhale the enticing aromas. Although most of him was made of metal, there was still enough living dog left to enjoy the idea of hot sausage rolls, cream buns, and freshly baked bread.

Dr. Borsch, on the other hand, acted as though he had no stomach and no taste buds, and certainly his nose didn't twitch and breathe in the lovely scents.

Having crossed the middle line cutting the city into the old East Side and the prosperous and bustling West Side, Dr. Borsch slipped into a maze of old brick warehouses and shabby homes joined together in long, drab rows. The sun, steadily raising its rosy face over the city, struggled to shed light down the cold, dark alleyways. Shadows lay deep between the looming buildings.

Something large and black ran across their path. Dog's head jerked up—a rat! He let out the whoop of his hunting call and would have raced after it if his master hadn't halted him with a stern command: "Stop! Heel, Dog. Leave it alone."

The rat stopped in front of a group of battered garbage cans. It sat on its haunches and waited for the man and dog to come along side it.

"Hello, Dr. Borsch. You're out early," it sneered, its long yellow fangs protruding from its mouth, its whiskers quivering.

"Good morning, Snout," replied the doctor coolly. "Have you any information for me?" The rat sat for a while as if it were in deep thought. Dog growled in his throat. He hated rats.

"Well," Snout finally said, "I did see a falling star last night."

He watched the doctor's face become anxious.

"Fell further over in the east, right over those old houses. They're going to be knocked down today. Probably very soon. Maybe right now, in fact," said Snout, darting off into some hidden hole and making a high squealing noise that passed for a laugh. A rumble filled the air, and the alley vibrated as if hit by an earthquake.

"What's that, Master?" asked Dog, cowering with fear.

"They've started a day early," muttered the doctor through gritted teeth. "I was promised the council would leave this area for another three days. Come, Dog, run!"

Dr. Borsch, scarf flapping like wings on a crumpled crow, lifted his long skinny legs and shot off to the end of the street. Dog crawled as fast as he could on his caterpillar tracks, built for toughness, not speed.

The black box bounced up and down as the doctor's feet hit the old cobbled pavement. Its low hum increased in volume as they went. By the time they entered the street that had once held Ghost Doll's house, the box was almost shrieking. The doctor dodged around the large machines, ducking and weaving, until he stood on top of a large heap of rubble. Dust rose around him like steam

from a bath, and the foreman was screaming for him to get out of the way. Dog trembled with apprehension for his master's health and safety.

"What do you think you're doing, man?" yelled the foreman with a large, ruddy face, dressed in a bright orange vest and wearing a hard hat on his head.

"It's gone!" cried the scientist in despair. "There is only an aura of it left here. Who took it?" He whipped around to face the group of workmen, standing shocked at this loony old man and his funny toy dog.

"Come on, Sir," said the foreman, lowering his tone to one of gentle concern, for obviously the old man was completely crazy. "There's nothing here for you. The houses have gone now. Nothing's left. Come on, Sam will take you home. It's not safe here." He escorted Dr. Borsch off the pile of bricks onto the level ground. Shaking off the hand from his arm, Dr. Borsch shook

his box, listened, and readjusted the settings. The frantic shriek became a quiet hum again.

"Of course," said the doctor. "It's fallen into a car or something. It's moving away, back the way we came. I should have thought of that and factored it into the equation. Come on, Dog."

The strange pair set off again, up the alley and back into the shadows.

The foreman and his crew stood for a few more minutes, shaking their heads. "Must have wandered away from the nursing home," said Sam as he hauled himself up into the cabin of his wrecking ball truck and turned the key in the ignition.

Chapter 5

The sound of the wrecking ball echoed down the road after Ghost Doll and Jasper. Dust chased them, covering them with a fine, powdery sheet. By the time they had put two or three streets between them and the demolition gang, Ghost Doll and Jasper felt the vibrations die away, and they slowed to a walking pace. Ghost Doll looked at Jasper, gasped, then laughed.

"You look like me, now," she said. Jasper was white from head to toe, only his two yellow-green eyes showing that he was Jasper.

"What?" he asked, shaking himself to dislodge some of the dust. He peered at himself in a darkened window and saw two pale figures reflected there. It was quite funny, he had to admit, and they both began giggling.

"Hmm," said Jasper at last. "Can't say it particularly appeals to me. Although it suits you fine," he added hastily when he saw the sad expression on Ghost Doll's face.

They spent a few minutes in the shade of a stack of cardboard boxes while Jasper did his best to restore his coat to its normal color. Ghost Doll peered up the alley.

"What's that noise?" she asked, as Jasper finished his grooming.

"What noise?" asked Jasper.

"That roaring noise. Is it the sea?"

Jasper let out a rasping laugh. "The sea? You are joking, aren't you? That's just traffic. It's rush hour."

Ghost Doll had a blank look on her face, so Jasper came over and rubbed against her, as much as he could with her insubstantial form.

"Traffic, rush hour. It's cars. People are driving to work in cars. Have you ever seen a car?"

"Of course I have," said Ghost Doll huffily. "My family had a car. But it didn't make that kind of sound."

They wandered up to the main road. Before they stepped onto the street, they stopped. Brightly colored cars of all shapes and sizes whizzed past them. People bustled along, carrying briefcases and umbrellas. Many of them held little gadgets to their ears and talked into them as they walked. Ghost Doll gazed in wonder.

"What are those things?" she asked Jasper in a whisper.

"What things?"

"Those little book things they have to their ears."

"Oh, cell phones," said Jasper. "Everyone has a cell phone. You can talk to people, text people, check your email and messages."

Ghost Doll stopped listening to him—it wasn't a language she understood.

"Look how short those skirts are," she said. "And those heels! How can they walk like that?"

"Come on," said Jasper. "We can't stay here. We can be seen by everyone. Let's find somewhere quieter to spend the day. But first, I have to get some breakfast."

They found a quiet park. Jasper delicately ate his fish head, scavenged from a bin behind a seafood restaurant, and followed it with a couple of cold fries. Ghost Doll watched him in fascination.

"Want some?" he asked, but Ghost Doll shook her head.

When he'd finished eating, Jasper had another bath, mostly around his face and head area. After that, they strolled across the empty green space.

"Don't people ever come here?" asked Ghost Doll.

"Not on a school day, usually," said Jasper. "It tends to get a bit busy around lunchtime though, so we'll have to hide somewhere. But we're okay for another hour or two."

Ghost Doll tried to swing, but her new starlight form made it a bit tricky to stay on the seat. She wasn't completely see-through and she wasn't completely insubstantial. She couldn't walk through, walls, for instance. In the end, she hovered over the swing, and Jasper, standing on his hind legs, gave the swing a push.

The monkey bars were better. Ghost Doll darted in and out and over and under the rungs while Jasper walked along them like a tightrope walker.

The sun was climbing to its midpoint. Jasper suggested they find a quiet, secluded spot to rest while people came and ate their lunches in the park. They found a hidden nook down by a creek, sheltered by tree roots and overhanging grass. Jasper curled up in a ball and closed his eyes.

"Are you going to sleep again?" asked Ghost Doll sadly.

"Uh, you got a problem with that?" he asked.

"I thought we could talk, that's all. And we need to make a plan, don't we?"

Jasper sat up again, then tucked his paws under his chest and settled into that sort of lounging position that cats do so well.

"We need to find you a new home first," said Jasper. "I wonder if we could find you a little girl." Ghost Doll glared at him. "Suppose not," he said. "I guess a see-through doll might be a bit scary for a little girl. We could find you a rabbit hole or an empty squirrel's nest to live in."

"Couldn't we find an empty house? I'm not sure how I'd like living outside in the rain and the snow."

"We might find a warehouse," said Jasper, his eyes closing with sleepiness in the afternoon sun. "I think I will have to have a little snooze. I'm so sleepy, I'm afraid."

Ghost Doll let him sleep. It was warm in the sun, and she had a friend. She had plenty of time to make a plan and ask her questions. The sun glittered on the water. A duck waddled down to the creek from the farther shore and launched itself off with a small splash. Ghost Doll sat and watched it, enjoying memories from long ago when she and her little girl would go to the park. It was very pleasant to think about, but also quite sad.

Chapter 6

Dog cowered in his kennel. Dr. Borsch raged about his laboratory.

"Where is it?" he shrieked. "Where could it have gone? It was there. It was there in that house, and then it was gone." The black box lay in pieces on the floor where it had been thrown and jumped on in the scientist's rage.

"Useless junk!" he said and kicked it across the floor. "If it had fallen on a car, we should have been able to trace it. When we got to the main street the signal stopped." Dr. Borsch strode up and down, trying to work out where he went wrong. Finally, he stood over his workbench and began to tinker with objects, tidying them up. Dog tentatively put his nose out of his kennel then crept over to his master.

"Maybe all those cell phones and computers interfered with the signal," Dog said quietly. Dr. Borsch kept fiddling with the things on the bench as if he hadn't heard. Dog was thinking of retreating when the scientist stopped and turned around.

"Dog, you are brilliant! Of course, radio signals, technology, interference. I need to readjust those settings. Good boy." Dr. Borsch gave Dog a half-hearted pat on the head before picking up the shattered box, pulling its insides out, and laying them on the table.

The signal was there, but it was very weak. The transmission was intermittent.

"Stupid thing!" the doctor said, twisting the knobs viciously. "Piece of trash."

Dog stayed out of reach. The doctor moved to the window and stood there for ages. The afternoon sun was setting, and long shadows drifted across the street below. A movement caught the scientist's eye, a tiny, sneaky shift in the gloom. Suddenly, Dr. Borsch whirled around, clapped his hands to his head, and exclaimed, "Of course!" He darted across the floor to where a rubber tube hung from a hook on the wall. It had a funnel shape at the end, and the scientist lifted this to his mouth.

"Good evening," Dr. Borsch said into the funnel. "Am I speaking to Trattorus? I think we should meet. I have a proposition for you."

///////////////////////////////////

"Jasper, Jasper." Ghost Doll tried to shake the cat awake. "It's getting late."

Jasper opened one eye and then another, stretched out one paw, two paws, then flexed them. He sat up and let his eyes grow huge in the dim light.

"Ah," said Jasper, "that's what I call a sleep." He licked his left leg and pulled a paw over one ear. "Right, let's think . . . shelter for you, food for me. Food first, come on."

Jasper stalked towards the streetlights, where the hum of traffic was still constant, but not roaring as before. He slipped through the back door of a store and meandered down a hallway until he came to a light-filled room full of noise. It was hot in there, and Ghost Doll crept under a table.

"Two steaks and fries, no salad," called a female voice.

"Here's the chicken soup for number five," called another voice. Feet went back and forth and around the table. The clink of glasses and plates made it necessary for people to shout to each other.

Another, more muted noise came and went as the feet retreated through a swinging door on the far side of the room. Jasper weaved his way around legs, rubbing his head and meowing piteously.

"It's Kitty," said a deep voice. "Watch it, or we'll tread on that tail of yours." Jasper left trails of fur on black trousers. A large hand came down and scratched his head. "You want some dinner then?"

Jasper hardly needed to answer. A bowl was put on the floor and filled with steaming chunks of meat covered in thick gravy. Jasper purred. Ghost Doll moved closer to the cat as he delicately chewed his way through the stew. When the bowl was licked clean, Jasper sat and groomed himself yet again. Splashes of gravy had to be removed from his coat and then his whiskers. Ghost Doll couldn't help thinking that although Jasper took great care of his fur, he still looked extremely mangy.

"That's better," he said at last, and with a farewell meow to the kitchen staff, Jasper sauntered out the door with Ghost Doll close beside him.

"You sure you don't want something to eat?" he asked.

Ghost Doll shook her head. "Where would I put it?" she asked.

"Good point," said Jasper. "Now, we need to get down to business. A home for you. Somewhere safe, dry, and warm. Comfortable and preferably with company—suitable company that is. Let me think."

The roads were getting quieter. Ghost Doll felt more relaxed. She was tired now. It had been a long, strange day. They drifted down a side street full of houses. Curtains were pulled across windows. Stars winked in the sky.

"They're so bright," said Ghost Doll, pointing upwards. "I've never noticed them before." Jasper stopped and craned his head to look as well.

"They are, aren't they," he said, then looked toward Ghost Doll.

"They remind me of you," he said. "Maybe you are made of starlight." Ghost Doll smiled at him and kept her eyes on the stars.

"I can hear them singing," she said.

"Come on," said Jasper finally. "We need to find you a home."

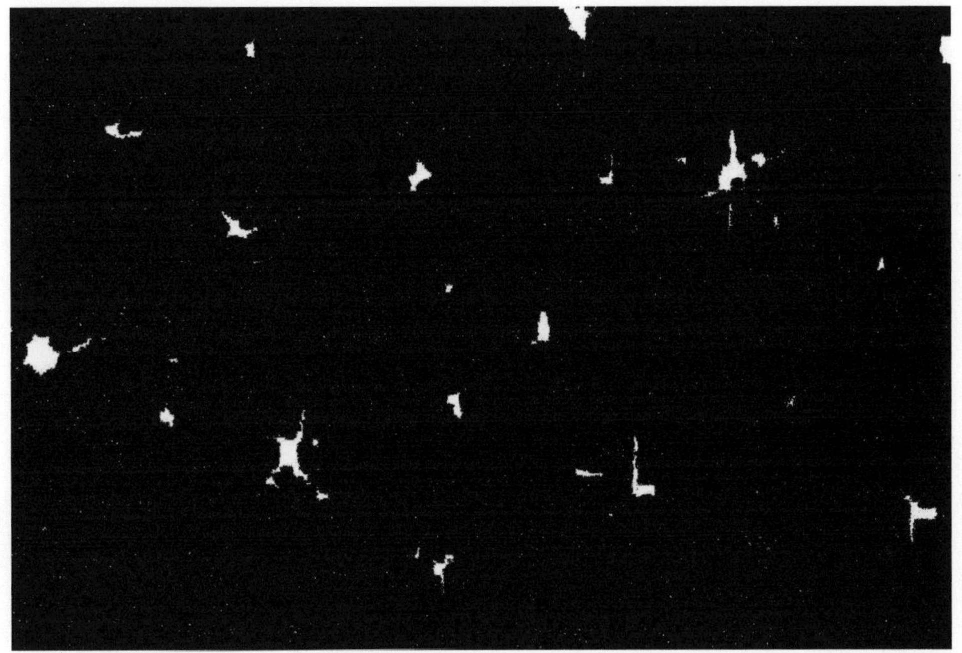

Chapter 7

In the dark tunnels and sewers below the city lived rats. This was their domain. They could hurry and scurry from east to west and north to south, all out of sight of the sun and the humans who would wipe them from the face of the earth. Close to one of their many entrances, a large rat sat on its haunches on a stone base. Its mean red eyes glowed evily, and its snout sniffed the air eagerly.

"He's nearly here," said the rat. Below it sat one hundred rats, silently waiting. "Let's see what he has to offer us."

Dr. Borsch ducked his head as he entered the tunnel. The walls were dripping with green slime, and he held a handkerchief to his nose. The rats watched and waited.

"Where are you, Trattorus?" asked the doctor, peering through his thick glasses into the murky dark.

"What do you want, Doctor?" said Trattorus, sitting up straighter so the scientist could see him. "We are busy and haven't got time to wait around for humans." Dr. Borsch bent his head to take a closer look at the rat king. Long yellow teeth and greasy whiskers quivered, taking in the man's scent.

"I need a favor," said Dr. Borsch. The rat stared at him with his piercing eyes, trying to decide whether this was a serious request or a setup.

"We're listening," said Trattorus, and on the floor a hundred squeaks backed him up.

"I've lost something," said the doctor. "It is essential to one of my experiments. I need your help in finding it."

"And what's in it for us?" asked the rat. "We're not a charity, you know."

"Of course," said the doctor. "I always pay my dues. What do you need the most?"

"We need medical expertise," the rat said. "Some of our best fighters are injured. There has been a rise in the number

of cat attacks lately, and our ranks are depleted with the dead and wounded. You are a man of science. We know what you seek and what you aim to do with it. We'll help you locate it, and in return you will give us something to make us bigger and stronger, so we can win our war with the cats."

Dr. Borsch straightened up, stroked his chin, and thought. "I see I will have to be more careful in the future about keeping my work secret. You must have spies everywhere. All right, I agree to your terms. You find me the stardust, and I will build you an unconquerable army."

The doctor put out his hand as if to shake on the deal, but the rat turned his back and scampered off into the dark.

"Well, I don't know," said Jasper at last. "I'm running out of ideas." They'd been walking for hours. There was nowhere he could think of that would make a suitable home for Ghost Doll. They'd looked in all sorts of places: backyards with dog kennels, chicken coops, garages, warehouses, and even an old car with no wheels. Ghost Doll had shaken her head at all of them.

"I can't live with a dog," she said. "They smell and have fleas."

Jasper had to agree with her on that.

"And the hens are noisy and they stare at you with those round eyes. And the warehouse? I'm sure I saw evidence of rats and mice in there."

"What about the car?" asked Jasper, but he knew what her answer would be, and he couldn't blame her. It had been miserable.

"Tell you what," he said. "Let's find a place to sleep for the night and we'll have a fresh eye on things in the morning." Ghost Doll nodded and followed him behind a pile of dumpsters. Jasper curled up on some old newspaper and went straight to sleep. Ghost Doll lay on her back and gazed at the stars. Their light was fading as the night gave way to dawn, but she could still hear their singing, faintly, high above her, and she wished she could join them in their great dance across the sky.

In the morning, Jasper said, "I've had an idea," while licking the last traces of cream from his lips. The empty carton lay on its side, wedged against a wall where Jasper had pushed it so he could clean it out. Ghost Doll didn't say anything, but she was losing faith in Jasper's ideas.

"You're a toy, right? At least you were once," said Jasper. "You are something a bit extra now, but essentially you are a toy; a doll,to be precise."

Ghost Doll nodded, wondering where he was going with this.

"Well, by my understanding, a doll belongs in a toy store, am I correct?"

"I lived in a toy store a long time ago," said Ghost Doll, brightening as she remembered her early life. "It was a beautiful place, and I had lots of friends. Then Lucy came. She chose me to go and live with her. Out of all those lovely dolls, she picked me."

"Well, I know a toy store where you'll fit in fine," said Jasper. "There are so many toys that no one will notice you're a bit different. Come on, I'll take you there now."

Ghost Doll eagerly floated beside Jasper. She was full of questions about the store: where it was, and who ran it? Were there many dolls in the shop? What kind of clothes did they wear these days? Jasper couldn't give detailed answers and finally resorted to saying, "Just wait and see."

It was around noon, and the pair spent the afternoon flitting from shadow to shadow when no one was watching. Several times Jasper had to push himself towards Ghost Doll to stop her from walking under someone's feet or into the path of a stroller. It was hard work pushing an almost-not-there friend.

It was evening when the pair arrived before a huge building of glass and metal. Lights flashed from every window, and Ghost Doll caught her breath at the wonder of it. "What is it?" she asked. "Is it a church?"

Jasper laughed. "No," he said. "It isn't a church, although by the way humans worship it, you'd think it was. It's the department store. This is where the toy store is."

Ghost Doll was bewildered. It looked nothing like the store she had been purchased from. It had been a single-story brick shop with a bay window in which toys were chosen everyday to sit and welcome children in. This was enormous.

"Is it full of toys?" she asked.

"Not quite," said Jasper. They sat together beside a sandwich board offering a special deal on hamburgers and fries. In the fading light they were hardly noticed; a mangy old cat and a soft illumination. People rushed past on their way to catch buses and trains. Cars honked in the snarl of rush hour. Lights flickered on in windows and the street. Gradually, the noise died away.

"Come on, the coast's clear," said Jasper, and he walked out into the empty road. Ghost Doll floated nervously after him. It was both exciting and frightening. New friends, a new home, new ways to understand. But what would happen to Jasper if she found a home at the toy store? Ghost Doll didn't like to think about that too much.

One long window of the store was filled with large colored pictures that were moving. Some showed people; others cartoon characters. Ghost Doll stared and stared. "We can't go in there, it's full of people," she said. "Why is it the same person, over and over?"

Jasper stifled a giggle. "That's television," he said.

"Oh," said Ghost Doll, delighted. "Lucy's friend at school had a television. I never saw it, but Lucy told me about it. She didn't say anything about how colorful it was."

There were still a few customers coming and going through the store's glass front doors. Music came softly from within. Jasper stepped up to the door.

"Come on," he called encouragingly. Ghost Doll hovered beside him.

"I'm scared," she said.

"It's okay, you'll be fine. You'll like it here. Now stay close while we get through the door."

Ghost Doll put a pale hand onto the rough fur of Jasper's back. It was warm, and she could feel a faint purr rising to comfort her.

When she was right in front of the doors, Ghost Doll realized they weren't like anything she had ever known. The door contained a circular box that whirled around slowly inside like a mixer. How were they to get through that? Surely they'd be squashed into paste like cake batter. Jasper felt her hesitate. "It's a revolving door," he said. "They take a bit of getting used to. Step in on the count of three and then jump out when I say. Ready? One, two, three . . ."

There was hardly time to blink before Jasper was saying, "jump!" Ghost Doll would have lost her balance if she'd been relying on regular legs, and as it was she kept whirling for a while afterwards. When she stopped spinning she was able to look around. Inside was like a palace. There were lights hanging from the ceiling in chandeliers and mirrors reflecting the many tiny little crystal light bulbs so that everything twinkled.

"Oh," sighed Ghost Doll, "it's a fairyland." Jasper purred louder, happy that she approved.

"We're not there yet," he said and walked off toward the center of the store.

"Moving stairs!" exclaimed Ghost Doll. "I've heard of them but never seen them. How clever. Lucy would have loved to come here." She floated onto the escalator next to Jasper, who appeared to be totally at ease, and they moved up to the next level.

The second floor looked like a living room. Cozy armchairs sat in little groups with coffee tables between them. Rugs lay draped over displays, and reading lamps made soft, inviting pools of light

across a much darker floor. On the far side were beds made up with white quilts and fluffy pillows. They looked very inviting.

"Can I live on this floor?" asked Ghost Doll.

"Well, you could," said Jasper, "but I think you'll like the next floor better." They went up another set of escalators and onto a floor already closed for the night. It was dark except for a handful of security lights and green exit signs. Rows of shelves loomed in front of them. It was too dark to see much, but they could just make out trucks and cranes, boats, spaceships, and train sets. All these were recognizable to Ghost Doll. Things hadn't changed that much after all.

"This is the toy department," said Jasper, waving his tail with pride at having brought his friend to the promised destination.

"Now, I suggest you find a nice snug corner and rest until morning. There will be time to meet your new friends before the store opens."

"You'll stay with me, won't you?" asked Ghost Doll, but she knew the answer.

"I have work to do," said Jasper. "A cat can't neglect his territory for long or some young kitty will take over. There are people to see and deals to be sorted. I'll come and see you tomorrow night, though, about this time."

Jasper could see the fear in Ghost Doll's eyes, and he felt unhappy about leaving her on her own.

"It's only for one night, then we'll see how you feel," he said gently. Ghost Doll hugged him as hard as her ghostly form would allow, and she watched him disappear down the now still escalator.

Chapter 8

A broken black metal box lay on the floor of a brick-lined cavern. Streams of rats came and sniffed it intensely before racing into the dark.

Each rat set off after the scent of the fallen star. The doctor had given them all an injection of a serum he was working on. It would double or triple their strength, he had said. It was a trial, and he couldn't guarantee how long it would last. The rats felt strong and brave. They couldn't wait to tackle the cats. But first, they had to find this stardust the doctor wanted.

They tracked the smell from the black box to the place the stardust had fallen, the now bare, flat block that had once been a row of townhouses. The scent was very faint. The stardust had moved on. It had gone west, back across the main road, through a park, and to the back door of a restaurant.

"What are you scum up to?" asked an old tom cat, his ears torn to shreds and a long scar down one cheek. "Buzz off if you don't want to end up as dinner."

"Watch it, you ugly old fur ball," said one of the rats. "Mind your own business; pull your head in if you don't want it taken off." Before the old cat could lash out with his paw, the rat had bounced out of sight.

Further down an alleyway two young cats serenaded their girlfriend. A fat rat jumped between them, and without missing a note of their song, the two toms pounced. The rat leapt to the windowsill and ran over pretty Queenie, the female cat, as she sat still. She whirled around with teeth bared, but the rat had run straight up the brick wall and looked down upon the trio.

"Got to be quicker than that," it said, spitting into the alley. "No more easy catches for you." And it had gone.

"What a nuisance," said one of the toms.

"Just let me at him," said the other.

"There's something fishy going on," said Queenie. "I don't trust those rats. Let's go and see Jasper. He'll know what it's all about."

They found Jasper outside his favorite fish and chip shop, munching a fillet of Perch with a side order of fries.

"Want a bit of fish, Queenie?" Jasper asked as the three cats approached.

"I wouldn't mind a taste," said one of the young toms.

"I wasn't asking you," said Jasper with a low rumble in his throat.

"Was just saying," muttered the tom.

"So, what's new?" Jasper asked Queenie as he sat back and licked fish batter off his face.

"Rats," she said. "We've just been attacked by a rat. It came out of nowhere, jumped all over us, and dashed off, giving us lots of attitude."

"And these two brave soldiers didn't protect you?" asked Jasper.

"To be fair, Jasper," said Queenie, "it was too quick. I've never seen a rat so bold or fast. It said something along the lines of 'no more easy catches for you' before it sped away."

"I think you are making a bit more out of this than necessary," said Jasper. He licked Queenie up the side of the head, and she flicked a paw at him to stop.

"We need to take this seriously," she said. "I can feel something isn't right. My instinct tells me we need to be on our guard."

"I'll have a look around then," said Jasper. Queenie got up to leave, taking her entourage with her.

"By the way, Jasper," said one of the young toms, "Old Murdo Nally has put a price on your head—dead or alive—so you better watch it."

The cat scampered off before Jasper could touch him. Maybe Jasper could go and see Murdo before Murdo found him.

\\\\\\\\\\\\\\\\\\\\\\\\\\\\\\\\

Ghost Doll wandered down the aisles of stacked toys. So many boxes, so many wonderful designs. She gazed longingly at the dresses on the fashion dolls and remembered the lovely yellow sundress with its full skirt and lacy petticoat that she had been sold with. Her tattered white dress was all she had now. No toy moved as she examined them. They all stood frozen behind their cellophane windows, not a sign that they could move or talk. Perhaps it was whatever new material they were made of, Ghost Doll thought. Perhaps there was no life in it.

On the third row she came across terrible monster-like figures. She'd never seen anything like them before. She'd remembered Lucy's little brother having a tin robot. She'd been frightened of him at first, but he'd turned out to be quite friendly, if a little repetitive in his conversation.

Some of the boxes had holes cut in the see-through plastic at the front. A sticker read TRY ME—PUSH BUTTON HERE. After a while, Ghost Doll gathered the courage to try one. She floated in front of a fearful looking reptile with open mouth showing large, pointed teeth. With all her ghostly strength, she pushed the button.

A great, angry roar echoed throughout the room and the heavy jaws opened wider before gnashing together. Ghost Doll nearly hit the roof in fright. She whizzed around two more rows of shelves to get away from it.

A window faced out into the street. Baby toys, strollers, and cribs stood before it, forming a welcoming nursery. Ghost Doll went over, still shaking. She sat on the wide ledge among photo frames, food bibs, and an assortment of rattles. She turned her head up to watch the stars in their nighttime dance. She sat very still and could hear them singing even through the panes of thick glass.

"Why can't I be like you?" she whispered, tears rolling down her, face. The stars shone down on her and suddenly Ghost Doll realized that she wasn't actually a ghost but a fragment of starlight. The tears still glittered on her cheeks, but she started to smile.

Chapter 9

No one had seen Murdo Nally for some time, but that didn't mean anything in particular. Jasper knew that his archenemy had a large territory to oversee, and he could be anywhere within it. Tiddles and Mopsy, the two ancient tabbies who lived above the empty bookstore, said they had heard Murdo had been in a fight and was a little worse for wear. Jasper decided he'd take that information with a grain of salt. It was unlikely Murdo had suffered any great or lasting injury. Even Jasper couldn't beat him in a fight.

By lunchtime Jasper was beginning to feel a little worried. It was unusual not to have heard anything about Murdo. He must have beaten some cat up fairly recently. But there was no news whatsoever of him or of any fight. Time for lunch, thought Jasper, and he made his way down the street and around the corner to the back entrance of Joe's Burger Bar. Joe was a cat lover and always had tidbits on hand for a passing feline. It was also a good place to get gossip from other cats.

Jasper was about to tell Joe he needed lunch when a movement further along the alley caught his eye. Rats. Jasper hunkered down and slunk along behind a pile of empty boxes. The rats were in deep conversation.

"And so I says to them, 'There won't be any more easy catches,'" said the smaller rat. "You should have seen their faces when I jumped on the old girl." The rats snickered.

"Don't give 'em too much information," said a large black rat with half its nose missing. "We don't want them getting an idea as to what we're up to. Be better to have kept yer mouth shut." He whacked the smaller rat on the side of the head and knocked him sideways. The smaller rat bounced straight back and forced the bigger rat to the ground, sitting on top of him.

"Don't tell me what to do or say," he said, sticking his nose into the other's astonished face. "Times are a-changing and the meek will inherit the earth." And with that, he bent and tore a great chunk out of the other's ear.

Jasper, seeing his enemies so absorbed in their own dispute, crept closer, thinking he'd pounce at the last minute and finish the two off with one blow.

His paw slipped on a greasy packet, though, and the rats caught sight of him.

"What you gawping at, fish breath?" said the smaller rat, blood dripping from his fangs. "Want me to do the same to you?" The larger rat crawled out from under his opponent and shot off under a garbage bag bursting with trash.

"Like to see you try it," said Jasper, still poised ready to leap. "What were you saying to your friend? What's this about the meek inheriting the earth? How are you going to manage that, shrimp paste?"

"We've got a secret," said the small rat, unable to keep his glee to himself. "We've got a new friend, and he is making us into super rats."

"Oh, yeah?" said Jasper. "And who is he?"

"He's a scientist," said the rat. "His name is Dr. Bor—" but before he could say any more, the large black rat had returned with re-inforcements. Ten burly rats jumped out and covered the smaller one completely. Shrieks of pain came from under the swarming heap of rats. Jasper turned away in disgust and left them to punish their own. He bypassed Joe's. He had more interesting and pressing things to think about than food.

The night was withdrawing; the stars had ceased their singing. Ghost Doll sat, upset, on the window ledge, wishing Jasper would come back soon. Why didn't these toys move and talk the way she and the other toys had in Lucy's house? If she was going to live here, she was going to be very lonely. As she sat she began to grow uncomfortable, as if someone was watching her from behind. She shouldn't have sat in the open so long, she thought. It would be awful if customers saw her. Slowly she turned around.

Standing a few feet away was a large group of toys. They stood inspecting her silently, not a friendly smile among them.

"Hello," she said. "I'm Ghost Doll. I've come to live here."

A large teddy bear took a step forward.

"Why?" he growled. "You're not a toy."

"I am," said Ghost Doll, "or I was. I fell asleep many years ago and have been woken by stardust falling on me. I think I'm a sort of ghost-star toy now."

"Well, you can't stay here," said a spaceman. "This store is for new toys only. You should be in a junk shop or at a flea market."

"Or at the dump," said another toy from further back.

"'Specially with that ratty old dress," said a fashion doll, haughtily. Her friends grouped closely around, and they began whispering and giggling among themselves. Ghost Doll grew pale. They were laughing at her. She was old and battered and unattractive. The toys were right—she didn't belong here.

"I'll find somewhere else," she said, cowering under the fierce gaze of the toys. She wished they'd all go back to their shelves. They were much better when they hadn't moved. "I have to wait for my friend to come, though," she added. "He should be here soon."

The toys talked among themselves. "Okay," grunted the teddy bear. "You can stay til your friend comes, but keep out of sight."

The group moved away, back to their homes. Ghost Doll stood by herself in the light of dawn. Suddenly, the store lights flickered on. The toys all raced for their shelves and within seconds were all back in place. Ghost Doll dashed for the cover of a bassinet.

"Hey, Charlie!" called a man in uniform. "What was that?"

"Where, Bill?" Another man in an identical uniform came to stand beside the first.

"Over there in the babies' section. Thought I saw something move."

The security guards looked towards Ghost Doll. One of them turned on his flashlight and waved it around, but the light from the rising sun made it impossible to see anything against the window.

"Must have been a trick of the light," said Charlie.

"Or a rat," said Bill. "Saw a nasty big one the other night in electrical." The two men strolled down one of the toy aisles, then disappeared through one of the doors marked EXIT.

Ghost Doll crept out from under the bassinet and slipped into a recess behind the service counter. It was well hidden from customers and the staff wouldn't look there unless they'd dropped something. Except for Ghost Doll, it was empty.

Chapter 10

As evening approached, the last customer left and the staff rang up the day's profits on the cash register. The lights went out, and the toy floor was illuminated by only the streetlights outside. Ghost Doll came out and found the shop deserted, just as it had been the previous night when Jasper had brought her. She was desperate to see him. The toys were all on their shelves still, and Ghost Doll hoped they'd stay there all night. She wandered back to the window to watch the stars come out.

"Well, how's it going?"

Ghost Doll spun around and threw herself at Jasper. Her pale arms encircled his neck, and she kissed him all over the head.

"I'm so glad to see you," she cried. "I have to go away. They don't want me to stay. They say I'm not a proper toy and that I should be in a junk store or the dump." Her starlight tears streamed through Jasper's coarse fur like rain, evaporating before they hit the floor.

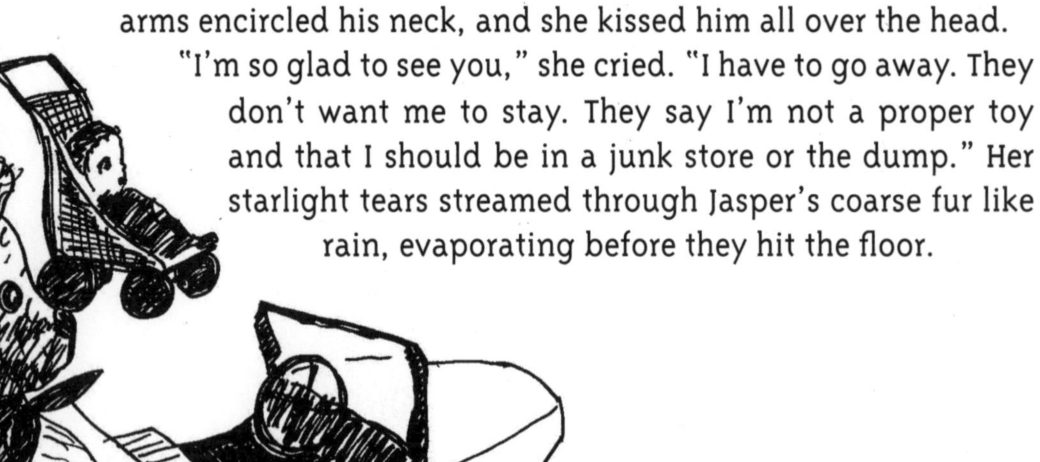

"Hey, it's okay," Jasper said, startled at the intensity of her greeting. "It will work out in the end. We'll find you a new home, not at a junk store and not at the dump. I'll think of somewhere."

Ghost Doll's tears finally stopped, and she sat on the floor next to her friend and poured out all her woes, including nearly being caught by the security guards.

"They thought I was a rat," she said miserably. "I must look very scary if they thought that."

"They weren't thinking at all," said Jasper soothingly. "But I will have to get you to stay here another night or two. There is business I need to attend to. Something odd is happening in town, and I need to get to the bottom of it. I think it's very important."

"The toys said I had to go today," gulped Ghost Doll, brushing another tear from her face. "They said I could wait for you, but then I had to go."

"Well, they'll have to put up with you for another night. It's not going to hurt them. What can they do to you anyway? You're more than a match for any of them. Lie low in a corner and mind your own business. I'll be back tomorrow night, and we'll get moving then."

Ghost Doll reluctantly nodded her head. Jasper stood up to leave.

"I'll see you to the door," said Ghost Doll.

After Jasper had gone, Ghost Doll wandered around the store. She floated down to furniture and spent time pretending she was in a real home again. But without children it wasn't the same. In ladies' wear she inspected the latest fashions. Those hoity-toity dolls upstairs should come and learn a thing or two, she thought, eyeing a full-skirted dress not at all dissimilar to the one she had once owned. She could sleep in one of the changing cubicles, she supposed, but that would only be until daylight. Surely there was somewhere in the huge building where people weren't during the day. What about the basement? There must be a basement in a place this size, she thought.

Ghost Doll floated down through a fire exit, past several doors, behind the boiler room, and through the storerooms full of merchandise waiting to be unwrapped and taken to the floors upstairs. There, in a far corner, half hidden by empty boxes, Ghost Doll curled into a small ball and closed her eyes. She'd go back into that long sleep she'd had before the falling star had brought her back to life. She'd dream of Lucy and tea parties and bright, crisp new dresses.

"What's this?" whispered a voice.

"Don't know," said another. "Give it a sniff, might be edible." A long whiskered snout edged forward and quivered over the sleeping doll.

"Smells odd," said the first voice.

"Like what?" asked the other.

"You take a whiff for yourself."

"Hmmm, you know what that smells like, don't you," said the second voice after it too had sniffed the doll all over. "That's what that black box the scientist had smells like. I think we may have hit the jackpot, my boy. Come on, let's go get our reward."

And the two of them scurried down the drain hole in the floor.

Chapter 11

Poor Ghost Doll, thought Jasper, as he left the department store. Those modern toys were really mean. He couldn't understand how having Ghost Doll among them was hurting them at all, as long as she kept a low profile and no humans saw her. He'd have to think of a new home for her. It was going to be difficult, but he'd do it somehow.

At that moment, however, there was more urgent business to attend to. He hadn't stuck around to see what became of the small rat behind Joe's Burgers, but he didn't think it would have been pretty. The rats were definitely up to no good. To openly taunt a cat was either extremely brave or foolish. And what was the name the rat had begun to say when the others attacked him? Dr. Bor-something. Perhaps he should find Queenie and ask her. She knew the names of lots of well-known people around town.

Generally, Queenie could be found outside the Sleeping Dragon Chinese Restaurant. There was a parking lot behind it that backed into an empty block where a house had burned down years before, leaving the garden to grow wild. Jasper thought it was quite likely she'd be hanging around there, waiting for the scraps left over from diners' plates. Jasper's tummy growled as he thought about scrounging up a nice Chinese meal along the way.

Jasper sauntered through the old garden. He guessed that it could one day be bulldozed to make way for more stores or another parking lot. The old fruit trees were covered with vines and the flowering shrubs had grown to the size of small trees. The long grass was brown now, and frost had killed any little flowers that dared to peek above the earth at this time of year. For cats, it was paradise—the perfect spot for singing love songs and wooing the girl of your dreams. Kittens ambled through it in the spring and birds made nests in the trees to bring up their babies. It was Queenie's favorite spot, and she always brought her own kittens to play there when they were young.

Jasper stopped to sniff a chicken bone beside a luscious honeysuckle bush. Not worth stopping for really, he thought, as it was already picked clean. As he turned away he thought he heard a faint cry, like something in pain. He pricked up his ears. There it was again. It was coming from beside the remains of the old brick wall. He stalked over carefully in case it was a trap. It might be one of Queenie's boyfriends wanting to warn away rivals.

Lying in the undergrowth, covered in bloody sores, was a young tomcat. It was Bernard, Queenie's only son from a litter two years before. The little cat, never going to be big and strong, was panting in pain. Jasper inspected him gently. The sores were beginning to become infected. And it looked as though he'd been bitten all over by long, pointed teeth.

"Hey, Bernie," said Jasper, licking the other's matted fur. "What happened to you?"

"They got me," whispered Bernard, his eyes closing at the warmth of Jasper's tongue.

"Who? Was it Murdo Nally?"

"Murdo? No, he'd never hurt me. I was wandering past the butcher's shop in Glenmore Lane. I wasn't doing anything but minding my own business." He gasped as Jasper pulled a lump of matted fur from one of the bites.

"Sorry," said Jasper. "Got to get these bites cleaned."

"'S okay," said Bernard, gritting his teeth. "Anyway, suddenly this swarm of rats came pouring out of a hole in the wall. They ran straight over me without even noticing, then one of them stopped and said, 'Hey, boys and girls, look what we have here! Let's give it the treatment.' They just tore into me, biting and tearing with their claws. No fear at all. They were so quick and so vicious. It was all over in minutes. Thought they were going to kill me, but suddenly another rat came scampering down the lane. It said something about he'd found it and they'd better help him get it before it got away again. They just left me and took off after the other rat. It took all my strength just to crawl over here."

"There's something going on with these rats," said Jasper. He'd managed to clean half the bites. It looked as though they had been made by larger animals than rats, though. "I'm going to go and get your mother in a few minutes. I want you to stay as quiet as you can while I'm gone."

Jasper gave Bernard a last lick, then dashed over the wall and into the parking lot.

Queenie's russet fur bristled when she heard what had happened to her boy. She called her maids and one or two of her suitors to go with her. "Thank you, Jasper," she said before leaping into the garden. "We owe you."

Jasper was very puzzled. First, he'd witnessed a bunch of rats attacking one of their own, and now this. He knew Bernard was an easy target for cats and dogs, but rats? Bernie was small, but he wasn't a bad hunter. He had stealth and super-sharp hearing. It wasn't natural that he'd been caught unawares like that. These rats were certainly different. They had powers that normal rats didn't have, and they knew it and were using it. He decided to go check out the hole in Glenmore Lane.

There it was, a drainpipe at the bottom of an old brick wall.

It must have been put there before proper modern plumbing. Jasper sniffed around the entrance, recoiling at the overbearing stink of rat. It must be one of their main doorways, he thought. He was too big to go down it himself, but someone Bernie's size could probably squeeze through. Not that that was going to happen. Thinking there was bound to be other openings further along the street, Jasper walked slowly down, nose to the ground.

"Ahhh, don't eat me!" Jasper nearly jumped out of his skin. Underneath his paw was the long, slimy tail of a terrified rat. It was small and covered in dried blood.

"No, you'd poison me," said Jasper, keeping his paw firmly on the tail to prevent its escape. "I thought all you rats were growing too big for your boots. I thought you guys had become supervillains. Unconquerable. Going to overrun the world."

The rat quivered pathetically on the ground. It looked ill.

"I've seen you before," continued Jasper, "in the alleyway behind Joe's Burgers. You were boasting about having help from a human, a scientist called Doctor Boring or something."

"I was punished for that," said the rat. "Should've kept my mouth shut. That's why they did this to me."

"I guess I'd be doing everyone a favor if I killed you now. Got any reason why I shouldn't?" asked Jasper.

The rat quivered, bracing himself for the fatal blow. "I can give you information," it said. "I can tell you where the doctor lives."

Jasper watched the rat squirm, waiting to see if his offer would save his life.

"Show me where he lives and I won't kill you," said Jasper at last.

"I can't. They'll kill me if they see me."

"Suit yourself," said Jasper. "Either they kill you later or I kill you now." He lifted his paw, claws outstretched.

"Stop!" cried the rat. "I'll take you."

//////////////////////////////////

"Here you go, darling. Would you like sugar in your tea?" Lucy was handing Ghost Doll a delicate china cup. There was a picnic blanket under the cherry tree. Every now and then white petals drifted down and fell onto the sandwiches and little cakes. Old Ted was there and Ginger the rag doll, Clown and Humpty—all

the gang. At last, thought Ghost Doll, I'm home.

She was taking a sip of her pretend tea when she heard the sniffing noise. What was that? She looked around her. Where were her friends? They were there a second ago. In their place was the face of a large rat. Its whiskers curved upwards, and it small eyes glowed a sickly yellow.

"Help!" cried Ghost Doll, but no sound came. She tried to run but something held her down. Fingers were poking her, pinching her, and scraping at her. Ghost Doll's eyes flew open. Rats!

Real, live rats were crawling over her, trying to get hold of her, to pull her along. She stared into the same yellow eyes of her dream and let out a very real, terrified scream.

"None of that, girly," said the rat with yellow eyes. "Come quietly and you won't get hurt." His taloned paw tried to grip her around the wrist, but it was like trying to hold onto sand.

"Not sure you'll be able to do that," said Ghost Doll when she realized they couldn't grab her. "It's a bit hard to hold onto a ghost."

She soared up from her hiding place and zoomed above their heads. There were an awful lot of them, she thought, and shuddered at the image of them crawling over her while she'd been sleeping. Thank goodness she was no longer made of plastic; they might have gnawed her to bits.

"So long," she called, and flew up the fire stairs back to the toy floor.

Chapter 12

Jasper was afraid the rat was going to die before they reached the doctor's house. The rodent was wheezing and gasping, holding a wound on his side. If it hadn't been a rat, Jasper might have felt sorry for it.

"Almost there," said the rat. He had a greenish tinge to him and one of his wounds was oozing fresh blood.

"You should get that looked at," said Jasper.

"Do you want to find this doctor or not?" said the rat, obviously in great pain, his energy draining fast. "I'm almost at the point that I'd like you to put an end to my suffering."

"Sorry," said Jasper and followed the rat in silence. They stopped at a grate in the outside wall of a warehouse.

"We get in through there," said the rat. "It leads to the cellar. From there we go straight up the stairs to the second floor. That's where the laboratory is."

"I can't squeeze through those bars," said Jasper.

"Tough," answered the rat. "Kill me now, please, before the others find me here and pull me apart."

"Too bad," said Jasper. "Tell you what, though. You scamper off now and I won't tell them who led me here." The rat stared into Jasper's eyes to see if he was telling the truth. Jasper's gaze was steady and cold. The rat turned and hobbled away as fast as he could.

It didn't take long to find the small first-floor window left ajar for fresh air. It led into a bathroom. Jasper landed neatly on the sill and slipped in without a sound. Second floor, the rat had said. He crept up the stairs, one light footfall at a time. A door was open enough for Jasper to slink through. He hid behind what seemed to be a fish tank. A man stood at a workbench. He had extra thick glasses on, and he was wearing a white lab coat.

On the bench in front of him was a line of rats. Jasper watched in fascination as each rat stood before the man and received a jab from a large needle. As soon as they had been injected, they jumped from the bench and took their place in a row on the floor. Jasper saw it was not just one row but several, and the rats were lined up like soldiers. It was the beginning of an army. An army of super rats.

A small, feeble rat hobbled up to the scientist. He whispered something inaudible up at the man, who nodded while he injected the rat. As soon as the rat leapt to the floor, Jasper saw it was the one who had shown him the way to the doctor's. He should have killed the little snitch when he'd had the chance because, Jasper realized, as the man turned his head towards the fish tank, the little rat had double-crossed him. Jasper didn't wait a second longer but fled down the stairs and out the window as fast as he could.

////////////////////////////////

"We thought you'd gone," said the teddy bear. "We saw the cat and then you disappeared. Why are you still here?"

Ghost Doll stood her ground before the gathered toys. "I can't leave yet. There is unfinished business," she said. "And I feel that I need to warn you of an imminent threat to all of you here on the toy floor."

The toys' mouths fell open. This was not the timid doll they'd made fun of the other night.

"In the basement," she continued, "there is a mass of rats." Ghost Doll watched as a shudder went through the toys. Rats were notorious destroyers of cloth, plastic, cardboard, and many other materials.

Ghost Doll did genuinely want to warn the toys about the threat, but she also felt a small sense of satisfaction at their fear. Serves them right, she thought.

"How many did you say?" asked a fashion doll.

"A mass, bird brain," said a robot. He reminded Ghost Doll of Lucy's brother's robot, although there was less metal and more plastic on this one—more vulnerable to breakage and rat teeth.

"And how many is that?" asked the doll.

"Too many to count," said the teddy bear. "We must prepare ourselves for an attack."

"How do we know they'll come after us?" asked a monkey. "They're in the basement and we're several stories up."

"Where there are rats, there's destruction," said the bear. "They'll find us out soon enough. Rats are always hungry. You can't rely on humans to deal with them. It'll be too late. They wouldn't notice until we'd all been chewed to bits. Rats will eat everything in their path. We must get ready."

The fashion dolls whispered nervously and rocked on their high heels. Ghost Doll felt a wave of sympathy for them. They were utterly useless and would be sitting targets for prowling rats. What she didn't tell the toys, and she did feel a little bit guilty about, was that the rats only appeared to be after her. If she left the toy floor, the rats may not attack the toys. Jasper would be here soon, though, and he was going to take her away. Then the toys would most likely be safe.

"Perhaps we should build a fort," Ghost Doll suggested, "out of building blocks and boxes. It will give us something to hide behind, and the rats won't know how many we are or what kind of ammunition we have."

"Amuwhat?"

Ghost Doll enjoyed the puzzled look on the other dolls' faces. She was glad that Lucy's brother had sometimes included her in his war games, as it was proving helpful.

"Things to protect us from the rats," said the monkey.

"Bullets and grenades," added a toy soldier, armed to the teeth with weapons that were molded to his body and therefore utterly useless. "Got any suggestions?" he asked Ghost Doll.

No time was lost in erecting a high wall of defense. Boxes from the storeroom were brought out and arranged in a tight circle. A gap at the bottom was left for crawling in and out of. Above the boxes wooden blocks were piled to add height to the structure. While the bigger toys built the fortress, Ghost Doll organized the others into collecting anything easy to throw: balls, baby rattles, packs of cards.

"We could use them like boomerangs," suggested one of the dolls and was rewarded with big smile of encouragement from Ghost Doll. They also pulled down packets of lollipops that were kept in racks beside the register for those last minute purchases by frazzled mothers.

"They can be used to distract the rats," said a small plastic dinosaur.

"Good thinking," replied Ghost Doll.

It was midnight by the time everything was ready. All the toys were huddled behind the barricade except for those on guard duty.

Three pairs of toys were sent out on patrol. It was Big Ted, the large growly teddy bear, who had suggested this. Ghost Doll liked the way he had taken control.

"Ghost Doll, can you accompany Monkey, please? You don't mind doing the first round, do you? We need someone with experience and common sense."

Ghost Doll was happy that he noticed her and agreed to go.

Chapter 13

No sooner had Jasper's feet touched the pavement than a door beside the steps to the warehouse opened and a strange metal creature appeared. Jasper was in awe. What on earth was it? It began to creep towards him on its caterpillar wheels. Its large metal jaws were opening and closing, emitting a loud, growling sound. Jasper stood gaping at the ugly thing, then suddenly realized what it was: a robotic dog. Jasper's tail swelled into a bristling spear, and he hissed in fear as the robot came towards him. He turned to run, but it was too late. The dog's teeth closed over the tip of his tail, and pain shot through him. Turning in midair, Jasper lashed out at the dog, his claws scraping against the metal. The dog's mouth was clamped shut over his tail. All Jasper could do was wail in pain and terror, hoping that someone would come to his rescue before the rats came pouring out of the laboratory after him.

A squeaking sound made him turn his head to the grates in the wall. Rats were squeezing through the bars. They were almost too big to get through. The serum they'd been injected with must have enlarged them as well as given them greater physical power. Jasper used all his strength to push against the metal dog. With a mighty heave he was free and running for his life down the street.

The night had not produced an attack from the rats, and before dawn the toys had packed away their fort. Now that they had built it once, they felt they would be able to build it better the next time.

The day passed quickly, too quickly for some who found the idea of a rat attack petrifying. Ghost Doll noticed that other toys were quite excited at the prospect of action and were eager to get everything sorted for the night. Some of the toys had been bought by customers during the day—the lucky ones, thought Ghost Doll.

Ghost Doll hadn't thought about Jasper for nearly the whole day. As the store closed for the night, she started to worry about his safety. He did tend to live on the edge and invite danger, and seemed to enjoy a good fight. Then she remembered that when he came this time he was going to take her away. Now she wasn't sure she wanted to go. All the toys had started to treat her with respect. Life might not be too bad here after all. Then she thought of Monkey, who'd been bought for a small boy sick in bed, and the fashion doll who'd been wrapped up as a birthday present. All her friends would soon be gone. New ones would replace them, that was true, but they'd always be leaving. Ghost Doll decided she would go with Jasper, but not before she'd helped the toys repel the rats. Jasper, would know what to do. He always did.

Jasper's tail felt as though it was on fire. He raced across a road, narrowly avoiding being hit by a bus. The vehicle honked angrily at him. Down the main street, around the corner, and into the ruined garden. He sat panting in the shade of an apple tree. As soon as he caught his breath he inspected the damage. Nausea overwhelmed him, and he was sick all over the ground.

"What a mess you are."

Jasper turned his head slightly and caught a glimpse of Queenie.

"We have to tell everyone," he whispered. "They're building an army." Queenie began to lick his head soothingly.

"I'll clean you up and you tell me all about it. Rest first, then we'll get the story straight." Jasper let himself be groomed by the rough but capable tongue of Queenie and let his story tumble out.

"I hate to tell you this," she said when he'd finished, "but it looks as though you've lost an inch off your tail."

"What?" yelled Jasper. "It was the dog. They have a metal dog. It's a monster."

"Let's get the others together for a meeting," said Queenie, coolly cleaning herself after having worked on Jasper. "I'll send out the messengers. We can be assembled in less than half an hour. Meanwhile, I suggest we get something to eat. You can't meet on an empty stomach."

Chapter 14

Closing time. The doors were locked and the lights turned off. At nine o'clock the security guards checked in on the floor but all was quiet. As soon as the fire door had closed behind the men, the toys went into action. The fort was reconstructed quickly; improvements had been made to the design during the day. The ammunition was piled ready for firing, and the patrols were organized. Ghost Doll teamed up with Big Ted and they talked quietly as they did their rounds.

"I think it will happen tonight," growled the bear.

"Why's that?" asked Ghost Doll.

"Got a feeling, that's all."

"You could be right," Ghost Doll said. "We just need to keep alert, and we should be okay."

"You still moving on when your friend comes?" The question took her by surprise, and Ghost Doll paused before replying.

"I think I should. You've all been very kind to me and I feel as though I could settle down here but . . ." and she told him how everyone else would be leaving and she would be sad to see them go.

"That's true," Big Ted said. "I've been here for six months or more myself. That's considered a long time in this shop. I'll probably be put on the clearance table in the Spring sale."

Ghost Doll didn't know what to say, but she thought he would be an absolute bargain and hoped he'd find a loving home.

They were making their third round, had passed the fire doors, and were going back towards the aisles when the door behind them opened. A flashlight beam swept across the floor. Big Ted fell sideways, but Ghost Doll was held right in the light.

"Get her!" shouted one of the guards. The second man dashed forward with arms outstretched to clasp her around the waist. Ghost Doll swayed to the left and the arms encircled empty air. The other guard pushed his companion out of the way and lunged towards Ghost Doll himself. Surprise had momentarily frozen her to the spot, but now she was zooming across the floor to the service counter and threw herself into the recess behind it. Two flashlights followed her progress and the men darted after her. Halfway across the floor a loud crash stopped them in their tracks. The fortress had collapsed in front of them, and there was no way they could get around it without proper light.

"What the heck?" said one of the men. "How did this mess get here?"

"Must have an intruder," said the other. "Might be kids hiding after the store closed. We'll have to call base."

"You do that," said the other guard. "I have a call of my own to make." They retreated down the fire stairs, each speaking into his radio.

Big Ted approached Ghost Doll, "They seemed to know about you."

Ghost Doll shrugged her shoulders. They had to do something before the guards returned. "We'd better get this cleaned up before they return with reinforcements," she said. "And, by the way, whose idea was it to knock over the blocks?"

A fashion doll stepped forward out of the gloom. "It was me," she said in a small voice, unsure whether she was going to be praised or yelled at.

"Well, it was a wonderful move. Well done," Ghost Doll said, beaming a smile at the nervous doll.

"Yes, good, fast thinking," agreed Big Ted gruffly. The fashion doll blushed with pride.

"Wasn't anything really," she said.

Queenie sat on an upturned crate. Next to her was Jasper, a rough bandage around his tail. Sitting, sprawling, and lying down were twenty or more cats. All of them had their full attention on the pair above them.

Queenie spoke up: "Listen carefully, as this could mean life or death for you." Everyone remained silent, waiting to hear what was happening.

"We've got a problem," said Jasper, taking the stage. "It's the rats." There was a slight snicker from the crowd, but one glare from Queenie silenced them.

"I know how it sounds," he continued, "but things have been happening and these are rats like you've never seen before."

"I've seen them," a small voice called from near the back of the group. Every head turned and saw Bernard sit up with difficulty. He told them how he'd been attacked and would have been killed if the rats hadn't been called away by another rat.

"So, what should we do?" asked a red tomcat.

"We need a plan," said Tiddles.

"A clever plan," added Mopsy.

"We need to present a united force," said Queenie. "I want all the fastest runners to spread the news. We have to get all cats on board, even those we'd normally never hang around with. Now, Jones and Turbit, I want you to take the streets between Cleveland and Rowley. Melanie and Sookie, you take the lanes behind the Bow Street stores."

Queenie kept giving out orders and the cats took off. The cats that were left began to organize themselves into groups. The old, very young, and weak were left in the garden directly behind the garden wall. They were told to keep quiet until the others returned. Bernard crawled up next to his grandmother, old Flora. She nuzzled him as if he were still a baby, and he nestled into her fur and purred.

"I have to go and see a friend of mine," Jasper told Queenie. "I think she is in danger. The scientist, this Doctor Borsch, I think he is looking for her, and I don't think he intends to be very nice to her when he finds her."

Chapter 15

"Yes?" Doctor Borsch answered the phone harshly.

"Uncle, it's me, Charlie, from the department store. I think I've found what you're looking for."

"Oh, right, can you give me more details?"

"I saw her with my own eyes. She's a doll, but she looks like a ghost. She glows. It must be the stardust. She's in the toy department."

"I'll be there very soon. You'll let me in?"

"Of course, Uncle."

"Dog, we need to get ready. Call Trattorus for me and tell him to meet me with the troops at the department store. Now it's time to try my latest invention."

The doctor took off his lab coat and hung it behind the door. He put on his old tweed overcoat and his hat. He wound a scarf around his neck three times. He then went to the workbench and picked up an object that looked like a gun and a vacuum cleaner.

"Come, my beauty. Let's go hunting stardust."

Jasper ran. His tail throbbed and he felt off balance. He must get to the store before the rats did. Ghost Doll probably didn't even know of the danger she was in. He ran across Taylor Square and darted down Greenway Lane. He was treading on enemy territory, but it was a shortcut. If Murdo Nally was lurking in the Lane tonight, he'd better watch out.

Jasper was about to turn into Main Street when a paw lashed out and gave him a ringing slap on the side of the head.

"What you doing on my patch?" growled a great red tomcat. He had a scar down one cheek and his ears had been torn to ribbons. It was Murdo Nally.

"Murdo," Jasper tried to say, but he was given another slap on the head. Jasper jumped to his feet, staggered a couple of steps, and fell over. Murdo was on him right away. His claws were out lashing and tearing at Jasper. His teeth sank into Jasper's neck and held him hard while his back legs kicked him viciously.

"Now . . . is . . . not . . . the . . . time," Jasper gasped between kicks. "Something's going on with the rats."

Murdo paused. "What you mean?" Murdo lifted his bulk off Jasper and let him sit up.

"The rats are planning an attack on us, on everything. They have super powers."

"You're full of fairy stories, Jasper," said Murdo, resuming his kicking. Jasper felt the breath leave his body with each kick. He'd never make it. He was in no state to battle Murdo and he must get to Ghost Doll. With an mighty heave, Jasper pushed Murdo over onto his back, where he struggled like a turtle.

"Maybe you should lose a couple of pounds, Murdo," Jasper yelled at the red cat as he sprinted off onto Main Street.

Chapter 16

"Do you think we're safe now?" asked Big Ted.

"I don't think so," Ghost Doll answered. There was more than one enemy involved and she didn't know which to worry about most. The rats were a threat to all the others but not directly to her. The guards, on the other hand, had recognized her and had tried to capture her. They would be back, she was sure.

"We need to be prepared against the rats," she said. "We must be vigilant. I think it might be me they are after. They tried to capture me in the basement. I think they would attack you as well. It's in their nature to chew and destroy."

"We'd better rally the troops then," Big Ted said and strode off to the toys standing huddled together between the aisles. "Come on, everyone. We need to discuss our plan."

Ghost Doll waited on the sideline. She was very uneasy and wanted to be on the lookout for any sudden movement. The toys were murmuring softly and giving her nervous glances. Ghost Doll tried to reassure them with a smile.

She'd just waved to the little fashion doll who'd pushed the building blocks on top of the security guards when she turned back to check the entrance. She caught a flicker of movement.

"Rats!" she yelled. Six huge rodents leaped among the toys and grabbed hold of a rag doll. The rest of the toys scattered in fright, all plans forgotten.

"Got her," called one rat to another.

"Let's go then," said the largest one, clearly the leader.

"We've got what we came for." The rats ran towards the fire stairs, dragging the poor rag doll by her long, blonde hair. She screamed and cried, kicking and thrashing about.

"Stop!" yelled Ghost Doll. "You've got the wrong doll. I'm the one you're after."

The rats halted and turned towards her. "You're bluffing," called one of the rats, yanking the rag doll so fiercely that she cried in pain.

"Look at me," Ghost Doll commanded, and she let herself glow in the dark room. "This is what you're after, isn't it? The stardust, it's here, inside me. Drop the doll and I'll go with you without a fight."

The rats hesitated, awed by the doll's radiance.

"Think she's telling the truth?" asked the rat in charge.

"Wouldn't be good for us to take the wrong doll back to the doctor. Okay, come over here and we'll let her go."

"No, we'll meet halfway," Ghost Doll instructed.

The rag doll was pulled along the floor. She'd torn a hole in her dress and her face had a smudge of dirt on it. Another one for the clearance table, thought Ghost Doll sadly.

The rats made a semicircle around their captive, holding her fast by both arms. The toys made their own semicircle around Ghost Doll.

"I will step forward to go with you, and you will release the rag doll," ordered Ghost Doll. She stepped forward right into the middle of the circle.

"When I give the signal, you must run behind me and to the safety of your friends," Ghost Doll said to the rag doll. The other gave a slight nod of the head.

"On the count of three you will release her," commanded Ghost Doll, shining brightly. "One, two, three!"

The rats, perhaps mesmerized by the doll's glowing light, let the rag doll go. She limped hastily across the floor and into the arms of her waiting friends. Ghost Doll also moved forward and into the circle of rats. She could hear the whispered assurances of the toys to their friend. The strange procession of rats and Ghost Doll made its way to the fire exit. As the door opened to let them out, the chief rat yelled to a group waiting on the other side: "Now, grab them all and tie them up. Light the fuse. We don't want any witnesses."

A band of rats charged through the door and before the toys knew what was happening, they had been surrounded and bound together with rope. The rats pulled it as tightly as possible, so no toy could escape.

Ghost Doll screamed and tried to turn back to help her friends. One of the rats was laying a long piece of string from the group of toys to a spot near the elevator: the fuse. Another of his crew was placing fireworks around the captives.

"How dare you!" she screamed at them. "You cowards!"

"Shut up, or we'll blow them up now," said the chief rat. "Come quietly and I'll consider letting them go. We need you to cooperate, you know."

Ghost Doll's light dimmed, she bowed her head, and floated towards the exit.

Chapter 17

"Where is she?" Jasper cried as he landed on the top step of the escalator.

"The rats have her," yelled Big Ted before one of the rats punched him in the stomach. He let out a low growl that ended in a wheeze.

Jasper flew across the floor, his feet barely touching the ground, stopping inches from the band of kidnappers.

"Stop!" he cried. "Let her go!"

"Too late, sonny boy," sneered a rat. "We got her now."

"It's okay, Jasper," called Ghost Doll. "I'll be fine, but please help my friends. The rats are going to blow them up."

Jasper paused, unsure of whether to follow Ghost Doll or rescue her friends.

In the middle of the toy department he saw a group of toys were bundled together. Ropes bound them tightly. They had all gone silent as if resigned to their fate. The rat with the fuse flicked his lighter on and off, taunting them.

The elevator door opened suddenly, and the tall, thin scientist stepped out. In his arms was a strange looking gun. Everyone watched as he and one of the security guards walked towards Ghost Doll.

"You've done an excellent job," the doctor said to the rats. "You have earned your strength potion. Now, step aside while I deal with this little problem."

The rats moved away, leaving Ghost Doll shimmering faintly beside the fire exit. Dr. Borsch raised his machine to shoulder height, braced it against his chest, and pressed a button on its side. A whooshing sound started and for a minute nothing happened. Then Jasper saw Ghost Doll wavering as if a breeze were blowing her around. Dr. Borsch pressed the button again, and the whooshing noise increased. Ghost Doll bent toward the scientist as if she had no choice. Jasper realized the gadget was a vacuum cleaner and the doctor was going to suck Ghost Doll into it.

Jasper sprang at the man, claws extended, landing right on his face.

For a moment the suction left Ghost Doll and pointed up at the ceiling. Jasper sunk his claws on either side of the doctor's face and bared his fangs to deliver a bite to his nose.

The man screamed and fought, trying to dislodge the angry cat with his suction gun. Then Jasper felt a sharp pain shoot through his back leg. He let go of the man to face his new enemy. It was the dog.

Then chaos broke out. The suction machine resumed sucking Ghost Doll toward it, the robot dog threatened to bite Jasper's leg in half, and the rat with the fuse held it directly in the flame of his lighter.

With one last, terrified scream, Ghost Doll disappeared into the barrel of the suction machine. The scientist, with a cry of triumph, ordered his dog to heel and he and the security guard stepped into the elevator and the door closed. Jasper yowled, but it was too late. They were gone.

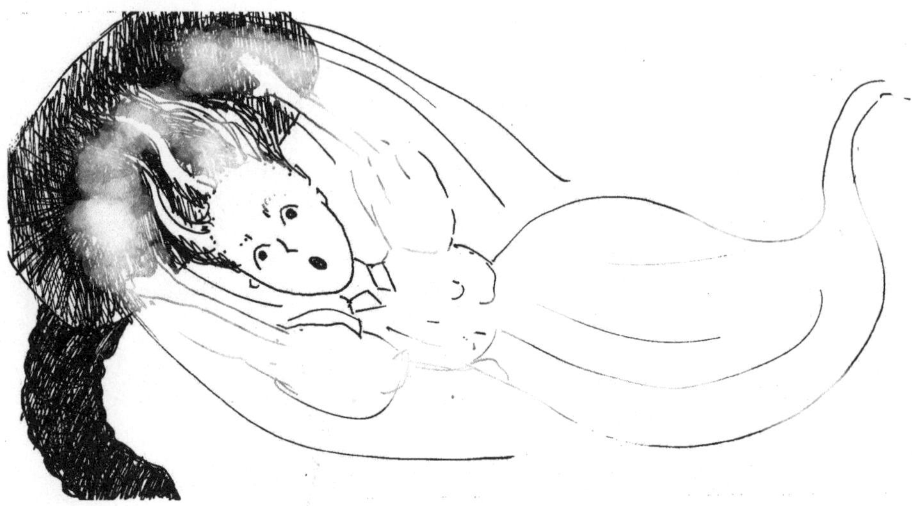

Chapter 18

Jasper would have gone after them, but the frantic cries of the toys made him stop. The fuse was burning steadily, inching closer to the terrified toys. Jasper ran over and pounced on the fuse, trying desperately to stamp out the flame. The rat that had lit it tackled him, biting him on his wounded leg. Jasper, already tired from fighting Murdo, feebly tried to kick the rat off. The rat's fangs sank to the bone, and Jasper howled. In agony he rolled over, leaving the fuse to continue its deadly course. The rat was on top of him now. His claws were aiming for Jasper's eyes. Jasper closed them and lashed out wildly at his foe. He was vaguely aware of the toys screaming in terror, and he could smell the burning rope. Oh, well, they'd all go up together, rat and all.

"Hold on there, Jasper," a gravelly cat voice shouted in his ear. "Leave this one to me."

The rat was pulled from the cat, and Jasper rolled over to see a big red-and-white cat fighting furiously with the rat. Jasper only had time to register it was his archenemy Murdo Nally before he remembered he had a job to do. The fuse had burned more than halfway towards the toys. Jasper took a flying leap and landed on top of it. The flame burned his chest, but he lay as flat as possible on it until he was sure it had gone out. Jasper took the fuse cord in his mouth and rolled over and away from the toys until he felt the end of it whip him on the nose. By the time he had unraveled himself the toys were cheering. Jasper saw Murdo standing over the now-limp rat.

"Thanks, Murdo," Jasper gasped, blood dripping from his face, his back leg dragging behind him. "What did I do to deserve your help?"

"Queenie told me what you did for Bernard. He's my son, you know. Bit of a runt, but that's not his fault. Let's get these fellas untied and then we have to rescue a friend of yours."

It didn't take long to free the toys, who hugged the cats and shook hands with them. Jasper tried to be patient, but all the time he was worrying about Ghost Doll.

Finally, with a last hurrah from the toys, the two cats fled down the fire stairs.

Chapter 19

The sensation of being sucked into the machine had nearly been too much for Ghost Doll. She thought she was going to be ripped to shreds. Not that she cared any more. She was too concerned about the fate of her new friends and hoped Jasper had been able to save them.

Suddenly, she felt herself being expelled from the machine. The suction reversed, and she shot out of the vacuum into what appeared to be a glass cell. She stretched, looked around, then tried frantically to escape. It was impossible—the case was sealed. She could see out of her jail into a white room full of all sorts of equipment: machines, test tubes, charts, and a large brass telescope.

The man who had sucked her into his machine must be a scientist; an astronomer, she thought. But what on earth did he want with her? Then it dawned on her. The scientist wanted the stardust. That magical stuff that had brought her to life. Well, he could have it. She didn't want it anymore. Her friends were probably cinders and ashes, and Jasper, if he was alive, should be allowed to go back to being a normal alley cat without worrying about her. She sank to the floor of her prison and simply waited.

"At last, my beauty," Dr. Borsch chuckled. "I have you. Let's begin the extraction before you can escape again." He pulled a lever and a sucking noise started up. It was different from the one she had just experienced.

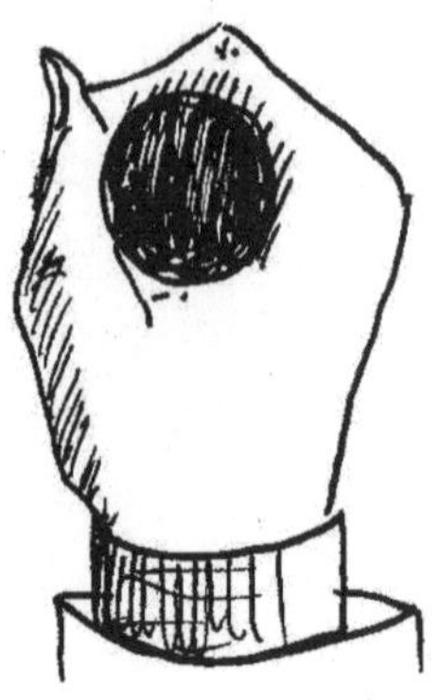

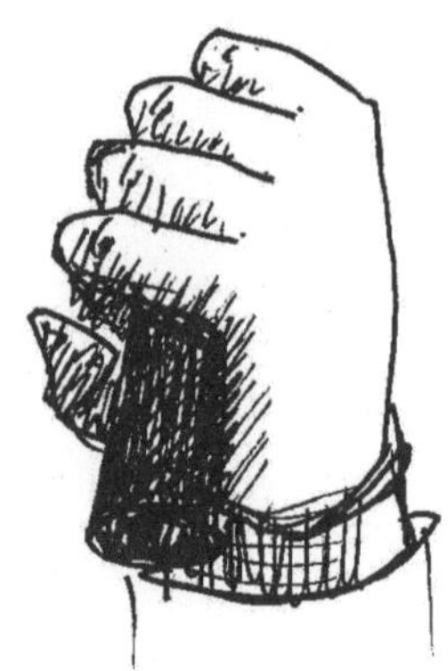

This sucking sensation was less forceful. She didn't feel she was going to be pulled apart. At first, she didn't feel anything at all. But then, after a few minutes, she felt herself feeling weaker, sleepy, and she wanted to lie down.

Another glass jar sat on the table attached to the machine and the glass case by a series of tubes. Gradually, a soft, sparkly glow could be seen in the bottom of the jar: the stardust.

Ghost Doll felt her frail plastic form returning to its mortal state as the cosmic dust left her. She ached all over. Her vision blurred, and she slipped in and out of dreams. She saw Lucy's face, bright and young, full of life, but then it changed. Lines formed and the child's skin sagged as she grew old in seconds. Then Lucy was gone, withered beyond recognition, and Jasper's furry form grew before her. She felt him nuzzle her with his nose, whispering for her to hang on, that he'd come and rescue her. But then he, too, changed. Ghost Doll remembered the metal dog chomping Jasper's leg. The cry of pain; the blood.

"Jasper," she whispered, "Look after yourself."

Then everything went dark and cold.

Just then a furry missile came hurtling through the doorway. It landed on top of the glass case. Looking down, Jasper could see his friend lying motionless on the floor. He launched himself at the doctor, who flung his arms up to protect his face. Jasper's claws struck out, and he fought like a mad thing, tearing and scratching, biting and kicking.

"Help!" shrieked the doctor. Charlie, the security guard, raced over, hitting Jasper with his flashlight. The blows were powerful, but Jasper was beyond pain now, his fury and despair kept him going. He'd fight to the death if he had to. It was Dog who eventually hauled him away, pulling him by one of his front legs. The other paw, digging into the doctor's neck, left deep furrows as it was dragged away.

Dog stood over Jasper and brought his metal jaws down around his throat. It would all be over in seconds. Jasper braced himself for the final blow.

"What the . . . ?" Charlie cried. Cats were starting to pour into the laboratory. They came through the door, and they came through the window. Suddenly there were hissing, spitting, furry felines everywhere. A sea of cats flooded the room.

"Call the rats!" ordered the doctor as he disappeared under half a dozen cats. Dog hesitated. Should he finish the cat off or obey his master? He couldn't see the doctor, but he could hear his muffled cries. Dog bounded away from Jasper and leaped for the speaking tube on the wall. He uttered one or two barks into it. Jasper crawled into a corner. His front leg was ripped open. Blood blinded him until he wiped it away with the other paw. He could just make out Ghost Doll lying still in the glass case. He edged toward the control panel. All of a sudden the rats arrived. Masses of them, trampling over everything, fighting and biting anything that moved, friend or foe.

"Get a move on, Jasper," growled Murdo, as he was choking a rat. "Hurry up and turn the machine off!"

Jasper pulled himself onto his hind legs. The pain was terrible, but he gritted his teeth. Reaching as high as he could, his good

paw touched the lever. With all the strength he had left, he pushed it upward. The sucking noise ceased.

"Now, push the button," said Murdo. "You need to reverse the process. Push the far button, then pull down the second lever."

Jasper felt for the button, shoved it hard, and scrabbled around for the lever on the far side of the control panel. He hung onto it and let his weight drag it down. The machine started up again and Jasper could only hope Murdo was right. A rat came out of nowhere and struck him on the temple. Jasper fell to the floor, unconscious.

"Where did all these cats come from?" Charlie asked. "And these stupid rats. Uncle, what are you up to?" The security guard had had enough and was trying to pull the doctor through the door. The doctor groaned, his face dripping with blood, his glasses smashed and hanging off one ear.

The rats, seeing the doctor disappear as more cats entered, gave up.

"This wasn't part of the plan," said Trattorus. "Even we can't fight all the cats in town at once. Come on, troops, retreat!"

As the rats scattered whichever way they could, the cats followed, pouncing and biting all the way. Within minutes the room was almost empty. Jasper's eyes opened and went straight to the glass jar. It stood empty of its liquid gold, but Ghost Doll still lay motionless on the floor of the glass case. Jasper's heart filled with dread. He'd been too late. She was gone.

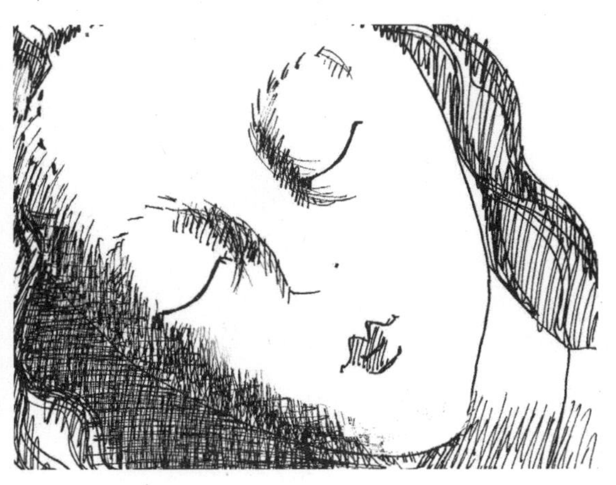

Chapter 20

Jasper limped over to the glass prison. He unlocked the door and entered. He lay down next to Ghost Doll and tried to lick her. She felt solid under his tongue, but cold. She had turned back to plastic, and her life spark had left.

Jasper continued to groom his friend, tears spilling from his eyes. The tears splashed onto her pale face. And as they did, a golden light began to glow through the fragile skin and warmth began to rise from her body. She opened her eyes and Jasper gasped. It was like looking into two tiny suns. He blinked. The next moment, Ghost Doll was up off the floor and had her arms around him.

"I thought you were dead!" she cried. "I thought you and the toys must have burned together." Her warmth sank into Jasper's matted fur and gave him strength. He sat up.

"Come on, you two," said Murdo, flicking a dead rat from his shoulder. "We aren't out of the woods yet."

They followed him out the door and down the stairs. The front door was open where the security guard had led his uncle to safety. An ambulance was waiting in the street, its lights throbbing. The doctor lay on a stretcher. He was still alive.

Murdo looked around and said, "I think it might be safer for all if you two left the city and laid low for awhile. The other cats and I can deal with this. Go on, before that doctor can issue any more orders."

Jasper tried to thank the big tom. "You owe me," was all Murdo said and waved them away.

Ghost Doll tried to support Jasper but her ghostly form could do nothing more than warm him. They hobbled down the street, trying to put as much distance between them and the doctor's house as they could.

As night descended, Ghost Doll anxiously looked for somewhere for Jasper to rest. She could feel his energy waning, and he was shivering. Finally, they found a garden shed in an overgrown garden. There was light coming from the nearby house, but it was obvious the occupants weren't good gardeners. However, inside the shed it was warm and dry. A pile of old sacks lay on the floor.

Ghost Doll watched Jasper sink down onto the sacks. He had his eyes closed, and his breathing was rapid and shallow. She bent over him to check his wounds. His front leg was gaping open, the bleeding had stopped, but Ghost Doll was sure it was infected. Jasper's face was a mess, and his back leg lay at an odd angle, broken for sure. She'd have to clean him up as best she could and let him rest. Maybe she could find him some food.

There were rags in a cardboard box in the shed. They seemed clean enough, so Ghost Doll spent a long time bandaging the worst of his wounds. She tried to straighten his back leg. Jasper moaned in pain, but when it clicked into place, Ghost Doll realized it had only been dislocated.

She left Jasper in a deep sleep and went to explore the garden. She floated up the back path and peered in through a window of the house. She could see a kitchen and spotted the remains of a meal sitting on the counter. With a gentle touch, the back door opened. Ghost Doll slipped through and looked through the scraps to see what might be edible for her friend.

"Jasper," she whispered when she returned to the shed. "I've got you dinner. Come on, you'll feel better if you eat."

Jasper tried to sit but couldn't, so Ghost Doll placed the bits of chicken onto the sack next to him and he ate what he could. He fell back and settled into a deep sleep.

The sun woke them both as it streamed through the window of the shed. Ghost Doll was surprised that she, too, had fallen asleep. Having your life force drained from you must make you tired, she thought. Jasper also sat up. He finished off the leftovers from dinner, then gave his face a wash. Ghost Doll thought he looked much better.

"We'd better get going," he said at last. "Murdo was right. We should leave the city and go into hiding. We need to lose the doctor or he'll be after you again. And we don't want those rats following us into the countryside. Let's go while they are still busy licking their wounds."

He hobbled out into the sun and Ghost Doll put her hand onto his back.

"I think we should head north," Jasper said.

Chapter 21

It took them two nights to reach the edge of the city. They rested during the day to avoid being seen. Ghost Doll became adept at finding food for Jasper. She slipped into a butcher's shop just before closing time and dragged away a couple of sausages. She waited outside a café until the scraps had been tossed out, then she loaded them into a plastic bag and hauled them over to Jasper, who was hiding in a nearby bush.

Jasper's cuts had closed up and his back leg, although weak, was able to move normally. It was the front leg that worried Ghost Doll. The gash should probably have had stitches. It was not healing, and the rags had to be changed every day.

The open fields, with their cows and sheep, fascinated Ghost Doll. She had once been for a vacation in the country, and she enjoyed thinking about it. Jasper, however, became quieter as they went along. He was talking less and his progress was slowing. His appetite seemed to be growing worse too. Ghost Doll was anxious

about finding food now that they were away from the stores. There was half a sausage left, wrapped in plastic and pushed into the sling she'd managed to make for Jasper's front leg.

Another day passed and the weather became colder. Winter had set in with a vengeance. They now slept at night, huddled together for warmth wherever they could find a bit of shelter. The clouds gathered and hung low in the sky. It was going to snow very soon, thought Ghost Doll.

Jasper finally finished the sausage but with great effort. Ghost Doll had to urge him to eat it all. He didn't talk at all now, and he limped along so slowly they hardly made any progress during the day. When the first snow fell, Ghost Doll had to push Jasper into an old, rundown barn. She piled straw on top of him and snuggled down beside him. In the morning she could feel heat rising from his fur but his body was shaking.

By evening, it was obvious Jasper was very ill. His thin body shuddered and his breath rasped in his chest. If they didn't get help soon, he'd surely die.

As night fell, utterly starless, the two staggered into the garden of a big old house. They decided to find shelter against the stone wall, but Jasper collapsed into the dead grass and fell immediately into a deep sleep. Ghost Doll put her hand over his chest and felt the bird-like flutter of his heart. Tonight was going to be his last. Ghost Doll looked around the garden. A child's toy truck lay on its side and a spade stuck up out of a pile of earth as if someone had just been digging a garden bed. People lived here, she thought, with children and toys. Light and life and love. Then she knew what she had to do.

"Jasper," Ghost Doll whispered. "I don't know if you can hear me, but I'm going to say good-bye now. Thank you for being my friend. Get better and live well."

With that, she bent over him and placed her delicate fingers over his muzzle. She let her stardust trickle from the ends of her fingers and watched as it fell into his open moth. Jasper stirred slightly. Ghost Doll's tears fell on his face and he murmured something. Ghost Doll bent her ear to his mouth.

"Don't go," he said. Ghost Doll let the dust run faster into the cat's mouth and saw a little strength return to him.

"Hey, Mom!"

Ghost Doll sat up, lifting her hand from Jasper's lips.

"There's something in the front yard. I think it's an animal." Porch lights went on and a door banged open. Two adults dashed into the snow, followed by two children.

"Where?" asked the man.

"Over by the wall," said one of the children. Ghost Doll slipped away from Jasper and hid behind a bush. A woman carefully lifted Jasper in an old sweater and, followed by the man and children, went into the house and closed the door.

Ghost Doll didn't know what to do. Could she find a way in and finish giving Jasper her stardust? Perhaps when the family had gone to bed. She wandered around the outside of the house. It was very big and old. It seemed as though the family were fixing it up. A ladder stood propped against one wall. New timber lay on the ground, and there were empty paint cans stacked neatly beside the shed.

Ghost Doll drifted onto the porch. The windows were closed and the curtains drawn, except for one small slit. Ghost Doll peered into the warmly-lit room. It looked so cozy inside. A fire burned in the fireplace, big plush armchairs were arranged around it, a coffee table was set with cups of steaming drinks, and there was a plate of half-eaten chocolate brownies.

Jasper lay on a big cushion on the floor in front of the fire. The woman was kneeling next to him, cleaning his wounds. The children watched from a distance. The man came in carrying a saucer with what Ghost Doll guessed was milk. Jasper was helped to a sitting position where he could lap it up. He drank it all. He lay in the warmth with food in his belly, his sores cleaned, and fresh bandages applied to his front leg. Ghost Doll smiled. It looked as though Jasper was going to be all right after all. She watched until the family had tucked a thick blanket around him, turned off the light, and went to bed.

Outside, it was cold and dark, and it was snowing again. Ghost Doll felt lonely. She needed a warm bed of her own. She went down into the yard and around the side of the house. There, halfway along the house, was a small door at ground level. It was not locked and some of the boards were loose.

Ghost Doll slid into the black hole. It was very dark, so Ghost Doll let herself glow a bit to illuminate the room. It was a coal cellar. It had

been cleaned out and used for storage. The wind whistled outside the door, but down in the cellar it was warm and dry. She found a stack of cardboard boxes and sank down into them. She was now sheltered from the weather, she was safe from the scientist and his rats, and Jasper was being cared for. Knowing all that, Ghost Doll fell asleep.

Chapter 22

Every day for two weeks, Ghost Doll watched Jasper get better and stronger. He was kept inside for the first week and hand-fed. The woman changed his bandages every day and put medicine on them.

One day, a woman in a van came—MOBILE VET CLINIC was printed on the side. Ghost Doll saw the woman give Jasper a shot and inspect his injuries. She smiled at the other woman and nodded her head. Ghost Doll knew she was telling them that Jasper was going to be just fine.

During the second week, Jasper was allowed outside to have short visits to the garden. The children were always with him, and he didn't stay out long in the snow. In the evenings, Ghost Doll watched the family through gaps in the curtains. Jasper no longer lay on a cushion on the floor but sat on the knee of the man or the woman. Ghost Doll could almost hear him purring. The children played games with him, teasing him with a toy mouse on a string. He grew fatter, and his fur started to glisten in the firelight.

"Jasper has found a new home," Ghost Doll said to herself thoughtfully. It was time for her to move on. It was no fun living in a coal cellar, and perhaps she could make herself useful in the world. Maybe she could help sick and stray cats. She would never go back to the city, but she might find a town further along the road.

The next day, Jasper lay in a patch of sunshine on the porch. The family had gone out for a while. Ghost Doll shyly approached.

"Hello, Jasper," she said. "How are you feeling?"

Jasper leaped to his feet and ran over to her. He rubbed his head on her face and licked her hands.

"You saved my life," he said, "and found me a new home. But I was supposed to find you one."

"I'm so glad you are better and that you are happy here," Ghost Doll said. "I've come to say good-bye. I think I should go and help other poor animals in need. I'll visit you from time to time and check that the family is treating you well." Tears glistened in her eyes and she turned to go.

"Wait," Jasper called. "I want to show you something before you leave. Come with me."

Ghost Doll hesitated, but followed Jasper through the newly-installed cat flap in the back door. Inside, the house was lovely. It had been freshly painted in light colors, and there were rugs on the floor and paintings on the walls. Jasper took her up a flight of stairs, then along a hallway with bedrooms on either side.

Ghost Doll saw a pretty room with

a floral bedspread covered in dolls and toys. They went up another flight of stairs. This time, the rooms were more formal and some of the doors were closed.

Then came another flight of stairs. These were narrower and not so nice. They must be at the top of the house, Ghost Doll thought, because the walls sloped as if they were part of the roof.

Jasper stopped outside a little green door.

The paint was peeling off it and it didn't look as though the family came up here much.

"Go on, open it," he said. Ghost Doll stepped forward and pushed the door open. The room was dimly lit by a small window at each end. It ran the length of the house. It was another storage room.

There were boxes with items poking out the tops. There were old chests with leather straps around them. There was a rocking horse in a corner. Ghost Doll gasped with delight. An artificial Christmas tree stood propped in another corner along with a box overflowing with holiday decorations. A painted screen divided the room in half.

"Go further in," said Jasper just behind her.

Ghost Doll floated along. She came to the screen and turned to Jasper questioningly. What was he showing her? He nudged her to keep floating.

As Ghost Doll passed the screen, her mouth opened with surprise, but no sound came out. There, on the floor in front of her, was a lovely old dolls' house full of little dolls and furniture. And floating cross-legged before it, about two inches off the ground, was a little girl. Her face was white as snow, and her pale dress trailed in tatters behind her. She lifted her hand to push strands of white hair from her face, and Ghost Doll could see right through it. It was the ghost of a child.

"Lilly," called Jasper in a soft voice. The ghost girl looked around at him and smiled.

"Jasper!" she exclaimed. "You are looking much better."

"I've brought you a new friend," said Jasper, rubbing first around Ghost Doll and then the ghost girl. Lilly looked towards Ghost Doll and cried out in delight.

"You are so beautiful," she said to Ghost Doll. "I've been so lonely until Jasper came, and now I have another friend."

Ghost Doll bent down next to the child and put her arms around her. The little girl put her arms around Ghost Doll and nearly squeezed her in half. "Are you going to stay here?" she asked Ghost Doll nervously.

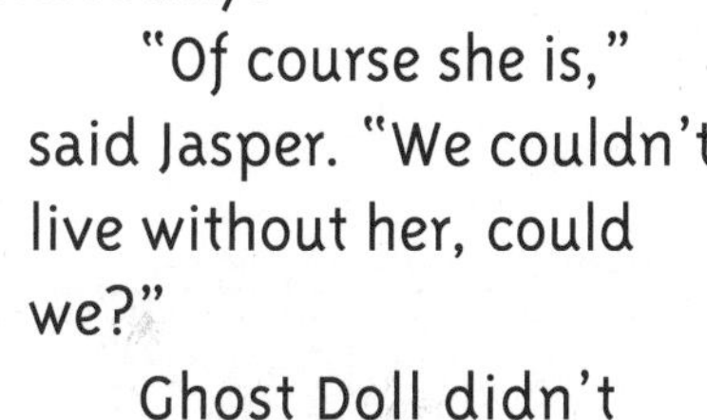

"Of course she is," said Jasper. "We couldn't live without her, could we?"

Ghost Doll didn't say anything. She felt the child's arms around her just as Lucy's had all those years ago. Everything seemed perfect. Jasper was safe, and they both had a lovely new family to look after.

After a while Jasper got up. "I think I will leave you to get to know each other better," he said. "And I think it's time for a snack."

With that, he sauntered out of the attic with his tail, forever a little shorter than it used to be, waving happily in the air.

About the Author

Reading books has always been one of Fiona's greatest pleasures, and from childhood she aspired to write and illustrate her own stories. After leaving school she spent four intensive years at the Julian Ashton Art School in Sydney, studying anatomy, life drawing, and painting.

On moving to the Blue Mountains these skills were used in developing her life-sized, oil painted cloth dolls. From sculpture she moved onto academia and studied Medieval Italian poetry, falling in love with Dante Alighieri, the long-dead poet.

Then, about five or six years ago, Fiona returned to craft and began designing knitted dolls. It was this that led to her meeting with Isabel Atherton of Creative Authors Ltd and the subsequent publication of nine books on various subjects from knitted dolls to a history of 1920s Britain.

Fiona lives in Armidale, New South Wales, Australia, with her family and pets. *Ghost Doll and Jasper* is her first published work of fiction.

Acknowledgments

Thank-you to my brilliant agent, Isabel Atherton of Creative Authors Ltd, who always has such faith in me. An equally big thank-you to Julie Matysik of Sky Pony Press for making a decision that made a childhood dream come true. And lastly, but never least, thanks to all those people who work so hard behind the scenes putting books together and making them beautiful.